T0365028

It's a
SECRET

JAYNE BELINDA ALLEN

authorHOUSE®

AuthorHouse™ UK Ltd.
1663 Liberty Drive
Bloomington, IN 47403 USA
www.authorhouse.co.uk
Phone: 0800.197.4150

Published by AuthorHouse   05/15/2014

ISBN: 978-1-4969-7981-0 (sc)
ISBN: 978-1-4969-7984-1 (e)

TENDER FOOL

My heart is such a tender tool,

Sometimes it can be a fool,

Sometimes it's full of strength,

It really depends on the length,

Of time it's loved and cared for,

And whom it calls out to be there for.

It hurts from rage, when it's engaged

With many, many different feelings,

Confusion creeps in, of where to begin,

Of what to say to her or him,

Sometimes it's best to stay away,

But when it flutters, and hears
tender caressing utters,

It glows and dances, and feels so young.

My heart is such a tender tool,

Sometimes it's cool,

Quite a calm and tender fool.

Written in 1997 by Jayne Allen

PROLOGUE

———⋈———

This is a fast moving, filthy, bloody, erotic, mystery thriller. The prostitutionalised eroticism takes place in Warwickshire, Mauritius, Greece and anywhere that takes their fancy. The victims are endless and the horror is prevalent.

Gerty lives her life as best she can, looking after her family and trying to make ends meet as a prostitute with a small time business. Her business grows but her family is threatened and moves to the lovely Island of Corfu, Greece. On this Island her desires to keep her family safe are dashed. She is distracted when she is snatched and taken to a church with surprising outcomes.

Her life goes from bad to worse when her son decides to get married but her Mr X hubby comes along and hots everything up to his detriment. Gerty is always trying to hold her family together but is betrayed by the one person she never expected. Gerty finds love and passion but is it enough to keep her on the straight and narrow? Time will tell.

CONTENTS

A Normal Life, Yeah Right!

———❖———

'Mom will you look after the kids? I got to go to work.'

Beth (Mom) replied, 'come in. Joe, take your coat off and John go tell Granddad he's late for work.'

John smiled with delight and ran up the stairs shouting, 'Granddad, Granddad you're late for work.'

Nan shouted, 'you got to get out of bed.'

On John's arrival at the bedroom door Granddad was zipping his trousers together and at the same time trying to find his socks.

'All right Joe calm down, stop shouting, I'm coming,' in a half-awake moan.

John ran back down the stairs as fast as he ran up. His Mom had gone to work and Joe was watching the telly.

Granddad arrived still half asleep and said, 'morning boys, where's your Nan?'

John said, 'in the kitchen and I am John not Joe, Granddad.'

Granddad said, 'sorry, you pair look so alike.'

John replied, 'ok Granddad you are forgiven just this once, you hear?'

Granddad smiled with compassion and walked into the kitchen.

Beth retorted, 'yes I have done your packed lunch, and your flask is over on the table, and yes go.'

Granddad kissed her good bye and said, 'thanks.'

As he walked out of the house, he shouted still half asleep, 'bye boys. Talk to you later.'

Gerty got to work on time and her first client was waiting outside for the place to be opened.

Gerty chuckled to Frank, 'you're eager aren't you?'

He replied, 'come on get 'em off. I've been thinking about you all night. I'm gonna show you a good time.'

Gerty said surprisingly, 'hope you got plenty of money?'

Frank grinned from ear to ear and could hardly hold his excitement, 'loaded, just loaded.'

The key turned and the door opened. She smiled at Frank and said, 'you had better come in then.'

As she was walking up the stairs, Frank was trying to look up her skirt.

She pressed her dress down to her legs and said, 'now Frank, behave. There's time for all that.'

'You got any knickers on then?'

'Of course, what kind of girl do you take me for?'

They roared with laughter and climbed to the top.

On the landing Gerty said, 'just go in there Frank. I will be with you in a minute.'

Frank did as asked and said, 'don't be long, my Carmen lady.'

'Bella where have you been, you're late again. Next time, there will be no next time. I need you to be here before I arrive. Your job is to see the clients before me and talk to them.'

'I gat trouble wid me kids. Me Mam is ill and me sista ave got a new bloke in, so she not lookin afta no bodi. Me bruva lookin afta em till twelve.'

Gerty said, 'I finish and you finish at four today. What am I supposed to do after twelve?'

'I go see me Mam and opefully she feel betta.'

Gerty was fuming and said, 'I need you to be here. I have a client waiting. I am going to have to find somebody reliable, Bella.'

With that, Gerty walked into the room where she had told Frank to wait.

There was another Prostitute called Prim. Her business name was Sassy. She was of an English rose white complexion, painfully skinny, tall, about five foot eight inches and her hair was curly, wavy and rich, a naturally blond-haired woman. Everybody adored her hair. She only worked part time due to caring for her Mother at home. She was due in later that morning.

Gerty was a prostitute and proud of it. She was a petite four foot nine inches high, slender, big-boobed woman. Her style was modern as in her hair was dyed black and cut with a straight fringe and her long hair down to her waist chopped in a subtle straight line. She wore her hair in various ways. Sometimes up and away from her face, other times up and thin plaits on one side but mostly she wore it down because she loved the feel of her hair dangling in front of her as she bent down. Her body was shaved from head to foot every few days. She would have a bikini wax done the professional way every end of month, in with her routine. She was very conscious of her role and needed to impress with her whole being. She would also have a facial, manicure, pedicure and body massage. Her clothes had to be good quality and she paid the price. Because of her height, she wore very high heels, which enhanced the elegance of her slender legs. She was definitely a handbag and shoe-collecting woman. Her nightwear was seductive, revealing and saucy but not sleazy. She paid the best to have the best. She liked her work and let everybody know about it. She was only discrete around her own family. She knew her Mom did not want her to do such a demeaning job; she also felt embarrassed about her daughter making out for a living. Her Mom thought it degrading and didn't want anyone to know. Word always got out and the rumours rubbed off. Gerty was not bothered what other people said and in some cases revelled in the attention. Her local name to whom she was acquainted was dirty Gerty but her working name was Carmen. She posted her nearly clothed, thoughtful, artistic, photos on her internet web page for her admirers and to help with business. On the whole she did very well. She kept her boys in designer attire and bought herself some serious outfits to go clubbing when she could get a babysitter. She had many boyfriends in her time but not all knew her day job. Some were proud for her to stop at home and play the role of wifey, wifey. If the relationship was serious enough from her part she would tell them the truth and depending on the guy depended on whether they stayed or not. Some even tried to come to terms with their girl being shafted by other unknown men while they were at her home babysitting her kids. Most of the time the relationship didn't last long as the relationship went only one way, Carmen's or Gerty's and that depended on whether she worked or not.

There was never anything normal about Gerty's life. She trudged along in her own sweet way, trying to do what was right for her family, work colleagues, and friends. Life with Gerty was always a mish mash of ideas, followed by the occasional action and surprisingly, a great deal of thought. She never did anything without thinking it through first. Unfortunately, like so many of us our hang-ups get the better of us and persuade us to stay safe. For Gerty it was a little of both but either way her life was a gamble and many times the challenge paid off. Not every time though.

This woman was a very determined specimen of self worth. She sold her body for more than a good price, lived well on the profits, and claimed her government hand out for her night out money. Wrong or not it worked well for her and her kids. The men in her life all had to work and take drugs. It was a past time for her to relax with a smoke of drug induced relaxant. The problem with that was the after effects the drugs had to her system and especially when she and the boyfriends had a big session. The next morning she could just about get the boys to school. Her work was everything and she made sure she was fit for that.

At about four thirty she arrived at her Mom's house, picked up her boys and went shopping. Before she left she gave her Mom a twenty pound note and said thanks for looking after them. She also asked if it was alright for her to look after the boys Tuesday, Thursday and Friday next week. Her Mom said that was fine and closed the door. Gerty decided to spend the rest of the day with her boys. They made cakes and watched telly when they got home. It was a good time had by all.

In the evening Michael, Gerty's new boyfriend arrived on time at her door. He was dressed in a flashy new dark blue suit with a white crisp long sleeved shirt and a multi-coloured tie but not too flash. His shoes sparkled with polished newness. Either way he turned out immaculately to impress, which he did. John and Joe glared with tongues almost tasting the air. The boys could see he was being invited in and sat down quickly in a, never noticed you there, pose. He was invited to sit on the settee and watched the telly with Gerty and her boys.

Gerty said after a few anxious minutes silence, 'come on boys it's time for bed.'

Joe and John raged, 'aaawwww Mom, it's too early. We're old enough to stay another hour, you said so last night.'

Gerty put on her stern glare and demanded with her body language that they needed to move or else. Both boys got up and walked there disapproving gorilla shuffle to the door at the bottom of the stairs.

Gerty said, 'say good night to Michael.'

They both blurted, 'good night Michael.'

The bathroom was cold, the bedroom was cold, the bed was cold, and putting on their pyjamas was chillier. Every inch of material goose bumped the skin and hair follicles with ice-cold raises of irritation. The boys quickly got into bed and put their side lights on. Gerty went up stairs to check what they were doing.

She went into each room and said, 'you can have an hour of reading but then lights out.'

With that little speech out of the way, she quickly skipped down stairs.

Michael said, 'I thought we were going out?'

Gerty replied, 'ummmmm, no, not quite. You see, I couldn't get a baby sitter.'

Michael smiled, peeled his pristine jacket off and said, 'Arrh well not to worry. I have you alone at last.'

Gerty snuggled up to him on the settee, kissed his cheek, and responded with a whisper in his ear, 'would you like a drink?'

She then pushed him away quickly as he replied, 'yes please,' as he melted like a lamb to the slaughter.

She moved seductively over to her new drinks cabinet, pulled down the front and took two Irish crystal cut whisky glasses out in front of her. She then went over with one glass and asked if he wanted ice. Michael replied quietly, 'yes please with a little ginger ale if you have some?'

The night was a tease from beginning to end and at Midnight Michael was thrown out. Gerty thought the only way to keep a man was to not have sex the first night but wait until she was ready to indulge. Michael was devastated but he was definitely coming back for more. He liked the goods and thought there is something he was prepared to come back for.

He blew her a kiss from the beginning of the front garden and whispered, 'I'll call tomorrow.'

She whispered back, 'be here for about eight then. Bye.'

Bella turned up unexpectedly at about ten o'clock the next day. She knocked on the door and Joe opened it.

Joe said, 'Mom's still in bed.'

Bella said as she barged in, 'I'll put der kettle on. You go tell er I is ere.'

Joe marched up the stairs, into his Mom's room to see his Mom open one eye that told him to tell whomever it was to go away.

Joe said angrily, 'it's your friend Bella. She said come down she is making breakfast.'

Gerty's face changed from one eye open to both hands on her pillow, behind her head trying to bury herself in her duvet.

Joe said, 'come on, you got to get up. She is waiting for you.'

Joe went back in his own room. Gerty slid her limp body out of bed and stiffly dragged herself to the bathroom, holding onto the occasional wall space. In the loudest of screeches Bella shouted, 'Gerty, git yer ass down deese stears, now.'

Bella was of Caribbean origin. Black as coal and a big Mama. Her Caribbean accent was very strong. Her heart was in the right place and always wanted to help even when she was in a mess. She always tried.

Gerty with a little bit more gusto got dressed into her relaxed attire. Sloppy jumper and leggings. No bra and certainly no knickers. She then clambered down to her lounge where she met face to face, Bella, wide-eyed and raring for a confrontational banter.

Gerty protested, 'you are not supposed to be here. You were fired. You let me down too many times. Go on, out.'

Bella moved around the lounge, took no notice of what Gerty was saying to start with, and replied, 'coffee?'

Gerty stood with her arm pointing towards the door in an authoritative manner.

'What ya tarkin about, girlie. Ya no fire no one. I com to tell ya mi sissy is lookin afta me kids while I werk wid ya on Tuesdy next. Tis all set now don't let mi down now.'

Gerty just stood in disbelief and said, 'I give up.'

Bella kept rambling on and repeating herself until Gerty totally ignoring what was being said, smiled in her face and ordered an answer, 'You having some coffee too? Come and sit down with me.'

They talked and switched ideas around for about an hour.

Gerty eventually shouted up the stairs, 'boys come on we're going out. Get dressed.'

Bella and Gerty's relationship had been mended and Bella went home. In daylight Gerty lived in a pretty clean and pleasant street. The neighbours looked after their properties which in turn looked after the area. It was a nice place to live, but the neighbours didn't know Gerty's occupation and if they did know what then?

GOD, IT'S THE VICAR

Gerty paid a visit to her parent's house. Dad was delighted and made a cup of tea.

Granddad said, 'how long have we got girls?'

Gerty said, 'oh, about a couple of hours. What you planning?'

Granddad looked at the boys and with wide eyes and a Cheshire cat grin said, 'how about I take the boys first to the park and then to a burger bar.'

The boys jumped up and down by Granddad's side and said, 'Mom can we, can we?'

Gerty looked at them both and replied, 'oh I suppose so but make sure Granddad behaves himself.'

Granddad said, 'I always behave.'

Gerty said, 'not what I've heard you don't. Go, just go.'

Grandma said, 'what about my kiss first?'

The boys kissed Grandma while Granddad put his coat on and kissed Gerty on the cheek. As quick as a flash they were gone. Grandma said, shhh, listen?'

Gerty whispered, 'what?'

Grandma said quietly, 'it's the first time this week the house has been so quiet.'

Gerty's Mom said, 'and how are you?'

'My job is great I saw . . . .'

Gerty's Mom said abruptly, 'I have told you before I don't want to know about your shenanigans, so keep shtoom. How is your new boyfriend? I here he's quite a catch.'

Before Gerty could answer, the doorbell rang. Her Mom got up to answer it and was amazed when she did. Her son with a beaming smile on his face was standing there. He was also in his uniform.

His Mom was elated and grinned from ear to ear, 'come in.'

She wanted all the neighbours to know her son was visiting. In addition, waved to one of them going past.

Gerty said in shock, 'well I never. Has he given you the sack or something? Or have you sent your notice to Jesus Christ?'

Lloyd said, 'now, now sister don't be naughty. I have come in peace and wish you no harm so put your horns away.'

He bent over and put his arms around Gerty and she reciprocated. Their Mom said, 'what brings you to the neighbourhood then?'

'I am literally visiting Saint Marks in Castle View and thought I would make my presence known.'

Beth growled, 'Gerty hold your tongue. Have some respect.'

Gerty went to say . . . .'

Lloyd said with a finger to his lips, 'ssshhhhhh child,' and smiled.

Gerty and Lloyd always had their bit of fun each time they met. Gerty would not talk of God and his church and Lloyd would not go near prostitution whether it be right or wrong. He felt it wasn't his place to judge. He just knew that he had a wonderful funny, caring and loving sister who he thought the world of. Gerty also felt the same way but Christ was another ball game in her argumentative state of mind. She would have loved to have had a debate at any time, day or night but Lloyd would never bite.

Lloyd's phone rang and it bellowed the song of the old Beatles song called Maggie Mae.

The song was all about a lady of the night (prostitute).

Gerty said in amazement, 'what a song.' Lloyd chuckled and replied, 'yes, it reminds me of you.'

He then walked into the dining room where he could talk privately. When He came out his face had become official, serious, 'I got to go and do some charity work.' Lloyd walked into the kitchen and told his Mom he had to go.

Lloyd quite sprightly, said, 'sister, I will see you again.'

Gerty stood up and threw her arms around him.

She replied, 'don't leave it too long next time, ok?'

He said, 'all right, but I really have to go.' With that, he wrapped his hand around hers and brought them down to her sides.

MICHAEL AND HIS ANTICS

Dad came home with Gerty's kids. They were exhausted.

Gerty said, 'look's like you lot had a great time. Dad what have you done to them, they'll sleep tonight.'

Granddad didn't answer. He just fell backwards on the settee and sighed a breath of relief.

Beth came in and said, 'anyone for tea?'

Granddad nodded, Gerty said, 'sounds good.'

The boys fell backwards, one by Granddad and the other on the single chair. Gerty went to help her Mom in the kitchen.

Gerty said, 'Mommmm, you know I have a new boyfriend and was wondering whether you would baby sit tonight so that we could go out on a date?'

'What time from, till?'

Gerty begged, 'is that a yes?'

Beth said, 'yes, what time from, till?'

Gerty told her eight until about twelve. She gathered up the boys and thanked her Dad for having them and drove home. Gerty had an old banger of a car. It was a burgundy Fiesta and did not match the image she wanted to portray but it got her from A to B and that was all that mattered for now. She also had not passed her driving test so she was illegal and wanted to keep a low profile. She kept meaning to take the test but first she needed proper driving lessons as the few friends, mainly men friends were teaching her for other favours that she was experienced at.

Michael phoned and said he was going to be late, about two hours to be exact.

Gerty said, 'the night would be over before it had begun at those hours.'

Michael said, 'there's nothing I can do, I am stuck in an emergency meeting at work and have got to go to it.'

Gerty angrily said, 'see you at ten then,' pushed the button to cut him off and threw the mobile down on the car seat.

The boys heard everything and said, 'can we stop up late being as Michael is not coming?'

Gerty said, 'no, you pair can tidy your bedrooms before you go to bed.'

Joe replied, 'oh, Mommmm.'

Gerty scowled, 'and you better do it faster than last time. John don't put your rubbish under the bed and Joe put your clean clothes in your drawers and not in the dirty laundry basket. I will be checking tomorrow and if you do it properly, I might, just might take you to the show case.'

With that, she pulled up on her drive and the boys got out asking what film to watch if they went out next day.

Gerty made the boys and her a light snack in her super dooper well equipped kitchen. She was a gadget girl and had every mechanical creation she could display. She made waffles with her waffle maker and some fresh ham and salad sandwiches to compliment her creation on the plates. She made hot chocolate in her hot chocolate maker and decorated them with multi coloured straws. She placed all the displayed plates on their designated table sections where their very own personal tablemats lived. She then tidied the kitchen to pristine condition to not a crumb in sight. It was possible she had a little O.C.D (Obsessive-compulsive disorder) because her house was dusted and vacuumed every day. The furniture had to be a certain way. Everything was placed to look fashionable and designer.

The boys had finished their bedroom chores and they sat with their Mom for their supper. When they had eaten, the boys were ordered to get their pyjamas on and go to bed with one hours reading only. Gerty tidied the kitchen yet again when they had all finished eating and went and had a shower, then got dressed to impress. She wanted to knock Michael's socks off when he saw her.

Her Mom arrived and Gerty had just finished putting her make up on. She scuttled down the stairs and greeted her Mom with a big grin. Mom had brought her knitting bag and put it on the coffee table. This irritated Gerty but she put up with it, not wanting to make a scene.

Gerty said, 'Mom, coffee or tea?'

Beth said, 'OOhh, errr, coffee please.'

Beth sat down and made herself comfortable. Gerty explained that Michael had to work late and that he would be late. Beth didn't mind.

Gerty said, 'how was the bus ride? Remember I am taking you back.'

Beth said, 'I know thanks.'

Beth got up and walked toward the stairs and said, 'I'm just going to check on the boys.'
She climbed the stairs, walked into the opposite room, and saw John the eldest looking at something under the duvet with a torch.

Beth said abruptly, 'what are you reading, John. Would you like some help?'

As she peeled back the duvet, she made John scurry for a hidden place for his dirty magazine but it was too late. Grandma had spotted the naked lady sprawled in a sensual pose across the page. John looked red in the face and could hardly speak.

Beth looked with a blank face and said quietly, 'you had better put that away and get some sleep.'

John gulped and shoved it underneath his bed then snuggled into his duvet. Beth crept out and whispered good night.

John whispered back still embarrassed, 'good night, Nan.'

Joe was in the same room and said, 'what about me Nan?'

Just as she was about to close the door she suddenly realised that voice was in the same room.

She looked around behind the door and said, 'oh, and so it is. I'd forgotten you were here.'

Joe said, 'I know. Good night Nan.'

She kissed him on his cheek, closed the door, and went down stairs.

Beth stood in front of her daughter and said, 'you look stunning.'

Gerty was gob smacked. That was a real compliment coming from her mother as she never gave her any compliments usually. Beth was ashamed of her daughter because of her occupation and wanted Gerty to know it in her own no worded way but tonight she was taken by surprise by her daughter's gorgeousness.

Michael turned up about ten thirty and Gerty was fuming.

His first words when she opened the door were, 'I am so sorry. I couldn't get away any earlier. Do you still want to see me?'

Gerty rolled her eyes in anger and stepped back for him to come in. He crawled through the tiny gap Gerty had made and he walked into the lounge. He introduced himself to Gerty's Mom and apologised profusely.

Gerty grabbed her coat, hand bag, and said to her Mom, 'I don't honestly know what time we will be back but I will take you home later, ok?'

Beth looked up from where she was sitting, then looked at them both, and said, 'have a nice time the both of you.'

His car was a Jaguar XJS in light shiny silver. The interior was dark grey to match the dash board. Michael opened the door for his lovely lady and quickly shuffled round the car to get in the driver's side.

Michael looked over as she sat ready for the engine to purr and said, 'you look edible, so gorgeous.'

She smiled with a half hearted gesture and said, 'come on then we're wasting precious time. I was not expecting to sit here admiring my driveway all night.'

Michael looked stunned and said, 'can we start again and just pretend I came on time and you liked me?'

Gerty looked his way and said, 'I will try but it's very difficult. You made me angry.'

'Yes and I have already said I am sorry.'

'Just this once but don't ever do it again, because there might not be a next time.'

'Ok, I get the message. This could be our first row.'

He pulled off the drive and waited for a gap in the traffic.

Gerty replied, 'one of many hopefully.'

With that thought, he drove off into their future together or maybe not. The night was a total success. They giggled, flirted, kissed, disagreed, agreed but the banter was extremely sexual. Gerty melted Michael in every way. She also took notice of other men staring and wanting more. She was hot wired for lust and tantalized all who pervade her space. Michael also took note of ogling eyes and found himself in a bit of jealousy. He wanted her to himself and she was spilling into the minds of others. Her radiant charm walked before her when she entered any room.

She asked him, 'have you a wife, children, gay partner, or are you single?'

'What gave the gay bit away then?'

'Just a guess. Well, are you?'

He replied as he put his elbows on the table in a secluded room, 'you know nothing and that makes you vulnerable, doesn't it?'

Gerty didn't answer; she just confidently let him do the talking. She had already fired the questions.

'I was married but am separated. I have two girls, one aged three and the other five. The girls are my life. I work as a Banking Consultant for W.J.A. Consortium. I was born in Coventry and at this moment looking for accommodation and staying with friends in their spare room.'

Gerty was very quiet and sipped her Disaronno and coke as her tongue played with the crushed ice in her mouth from the glass. He did not ask Gerty any questions. Maybe he thought she was a house wife looking after her two sons. He knew she was on her own.

She glared at his tie and asked, 'is that electric blue nail varnish I see as a design on your tie and speckles of blood on your shirt?'

'Ummmmm, yes why do you ask?'

Gerty smirked and replied, 'from your wife no dought?'

He seriously did not like the innuendo and quietly answered, 'it's from my mate's girlfriend that I am currently sharing the flat with. She fell on me and the bloody nail varnish went everywhere. I was late enough and so did not have time to change again.'

'What about the blood on your shirt?'

He did not answer. Gerty suddenly felt mean and adjusted her seat, then drank a little more.

After a minutes silence she said, 'would you make love to me in your XJS.'

He said as he moved forward to kiss her from the other side of the small table, 'I would love to.'

'Tell me what you would do.'

'Come with me and I'll show you.'

Michael called the waiter over and he paid the bill. He then stood up, helped her with her coat, and kissed her neck. They both moved hand in hand out of the pub and into the car park. He kissed her by the car and leant her body backwards against the side of his XJS. Her legs were stretched backwards and he pushed his body against hers.

He lifted her arms above her head and said, 'can you feel that?'

She went to put her hands down so she could feel the bulge in his pants but he held her arms high.

He whispered, 'you might be able to touch it later but for now it's throbbing for your attention.'

They carried on kissing. She ached all over with desire, emotion of uncontrollable passion. He could have had her there and then. It got to a peak where she didn't care. Her whole being was outrageously, crying out for more. Michael's hands let her go and he reached for the door of the car. He opened it and pushed her even more into his body, then he quickly backed away.

He then said, abruptly, 'come on get in I want to take you for a ride.'

Gerty could hardly stand but managed to collect her thoughts. She had not felt like this for a long time. In fact not since she first met John and Joes Dad many, many years ago.

In the passenger side of the car, she grabbed hold of Michael's bulging mass, undid his zipper, and crawled her fingers into his under pants whilst he was trying to concentrate on driving. She could feel the hard throbbing flesh and started to massage. His bell end would hardly fit into her palm it was so huge. Michael had problems concentrating and pulled into a secluded lay-by. It was pitch black with silhouetted trees and bushes. Everything in the car was electrical. He wound down the seating and created a bed like arrangement. With Gerty having his knob in her hand he carefully manoeuvred them to the back seat. Gerty was trying to get his trousers off. Michael undid her blouse and popped out one of her voluptuous breasts.

His tongue and his teeth played passionate sexual sensations with her nipples and he rubbed gently up the inside of her legs with the other hand. He stopped sucking her one breast and with both hands crept up the side of her thighs with the material of her dress. He then came down with her departing G string. He got her into position for full penetration and pushed. There was an instant overwhelming pleasure from both and then the repetitive pushing and pulling took over. It happened so naturally. They both knew what to do and how the best way would affect each other. Gerty gave a performance but this time she felt everything. Michael was not a client but something or somebody she could passionately relate to. She made noises and orgasmed for ever. From her perspective it was an unusual feeling. A feeling she had not had for years. This was not a job but the real thing. Their passions spilled over for quite a long time until their climax had finally arrived. Their bodies were limp and so were their minds.

After a few minutes Gerty said, 'is that it?'

Michael laughed and said, 'you cheeky bitch. Will I see you tomorrow or has that put you off?'

Gerty got hold off his hand, held it to her mouth, and kissed it.

'Can we do it again?'

Michael laughingly horrified picked himself up, got himself dressed and said, 'lady you need to go home. You are wearing me out.'

Gerty adjusted her attire and put some more lippy on. Once back to the way they were dressed and all prim and proper they drove to Gerty's house. He pulled up on the drive.

'Don't come in. What time tomorrow?'

'I will be promptly here at about eight if that is alright with you?'

Gerty kissed him on the cheek and replied that would be nice. She got out of the car and waved him off.

Gerty took her Mom home and when she returned went straight to bed. Sunday was a slopping around, do as you like day. The boys watched telly or played on their X box games. Gerty did house work and put it in pristine, sparkling condition as per usual. Michael turned up of the night time just in the nick of time so that he was not late. That pleased Gerty and they went straight to her bed. The next morning Michael went to work and Gerty went shopping. Michael was told by Gerty that she had art classes of an evening and in the day helped her friend with her shop that she owned. It was all lies but Gerty had to cover her tracks.

Gerty saw Michael practically every night or parts of the day. Their relationship was getting very serious. One fine day when the snow was no more and the spring flowers popped to say, hi world we are here to wake up the warmer days, Michael proposed marriage to Gerty, and she accepted. Gerty told her parents and they were over the moon with the good news.

After a while, Gerty noticed that some days he was unable to see her because of his friends that he stayed with, for what he would call a boys night in. These boys' nights in came to be more and regular. It made Gerty suspicious and he had him followed. Tension between them was apparent and little niggles of arguments crept in. A couple of nights later she had not seen Michael, which was unusual. They had been seeing each other for over a year nearly. Her spies told her that he was still seeing his ex-wife and his two girls. Michael had discussed the girls but said he did not see them because his ex would not let him. When confronted with this news he told Gerty he had been trying to get his ex persuaded so that he could have access to his girls.

He said, 'I have been seeing them regularly now for over a month.'

'Why didn't you tell me?'

'I was trying to make it work and permanent before I said anything.'

Gerty accepted this and loved him even more for his deceit. After a few months more she noticed he smelt of somebody else's perfume and the usual cliché of lipstick on the collar. All the classic signs were there for him having an affair. She had him watched again by her trusted friend. The information came back that he was having an affair with a tall, blond healthily tanned woman. He was seen leaving a hotel. He had also been seen leaving that hotel a number of times during the afternoon when he was supposed to be at work. Gerty confronted him again and this time He was furious. Furious to have been watched, furious to have his privacy invaded by a jealous woman and horrified that he was not trusted. He told her that she was a business partner and that they were trying to set up their own private company outside of the one they separately both worked for.

Gerty asked, 'why didn't you bring her home here so that you could do things behind our closed doors?'

'I don't mix business with pleasure.'

Gerty was not a stupid woman but he was so plausible. She wanted to believe him and didn't want to lose him.

GERTY MESSED UP BIG TIME

———❧———

After many disturbing months ahead, their lives started to settle down to normality again.

A knock came at the door. Michael answered it. There was a rough looking twenty five year old with cut off jeans and a red tee shirt on and a black bomber jacket over him.

He said, 'is Carmen in, I know she lives here?'

Gerty heard the name and worryingly ran to the door.

She looked at Michael and said, 'it's all right I will handle this.'

Michael looked highly suspicious but walked away into the lounge.

The man said, 'high sexy Carmen; Frank said you would see me for a quick one.'

Gerty said quietly, 'Frank was wrong go home and don't come to my door again. I don't do house calls.'

As she pushed him away she was looking back to see if Michael could see or hear anything. The man said with a whispered voice, 'sorry, you got another client. I'll come back later.'

'No you won't. You've been drinking. Go home and sober up and don't come round here again.'

The man said sadly, 'noooo, don't be like that, I only wanted a quickie.'

Gerty pushed him to the edge of her front garden and replied, 'I don't do quickies. Call the usual number. I will see you then.'

He apologised and went on his way.

Michael heard everything and grabbed his coat and left. Gerty stood there not knowing what to do. He slammed the door, his tyres screeched as they left the front garden tarmac, missing an oncoming van by inches. The van driver bibbed his horn furiously and Michael sped off. Gerty walked to the door with tears in her eyes. She closed it and stood behind gushing with tears that smudged her make-up.

WORK AS USUAL

When Tuesday came, Gerty dropped the kids off at her Mom's. She never told anybody about that night. She was hoping he would forgive her and come back.

At work a new girl was introduced to the routine of prostitution. She was a tiny frail little thing. She came from Bangkok and was forcefully brought into England then sold as a sex slave. She finally broke free from the clutches of those men responsible but did not know what to do. She decided to go back into prostitution but on her terms and that was when she met Gerty.

Gerty asked the girl, 'what name would you like to be known as, your working name that is?'

The girl replied, 'Chelsea.'

Gerty asked, 'why Chelsea?'

The girl replied, 'because I support the football team and I would like to be loved by every one of them, after they pay me millions of course.'

Gerty smiled and said, 'naughty. The money was cash in hand. Money earned was money kept and not divulged. You will have to pay ten percent to the receptionist in the building. She is your helper, security, and go getter.'

Gerty showed her to her new office and she got to work right away. Gerty worked next door. Their offices were palatial. King-size beds, side cabinets, wardrobe full of dominant gadgets for their pleasures, a suitcase for chains and whips, a dressing table and chair. The rooms were not only furnished tastefully, they also had very expensive bed linen, curtains and cushions for their pleasures. It set the scene for a high quality good time to suit all tastes.

Bella was working too and she was on time. Work was regular and running smoothly.

They had regular clients and regular times of opening.

A man was booked in that they did not recognise.

Gerty said, 'Do you have the cameras on?'

Bella said, 'yes, Ma'am.'

Gerty enquired, 'you have the police line just in case?'

'I sure do. Me brudder gev mi dis baseball bat. He bought it from New Yark when he on holidy der. I is ready.'

Gerty was optimistic and quietly said, 'you see any trouble, you call me.'

Bella said, yes, Ma'am.'

The man never showed. Gerty was so relieved. Months went by with no problem.

A LUNCHTIME TREAT

———◈———

Gerty asked her Mom on one of her visits would she like to go to Warwick shopping for the day, by themselves. Beth liked the idea and agreed. Gerty picked her up in her new car that Michael had bought her before they fell out. It was Ford Focus sport, brand new and never been used. It was painted black with black interior. Michael did not know that Gerty had not passed her driving test. Beth chose to ignore the fact. She thought her daughter was a nifty little driver and as capable as the others on the road.

Warwick was hectic with masses of people in every direction. Finally, they sat down after walking what seemed for miles around the town.

Gerty said, 'Mom, my treat, what do you want for lunch?'

Before she said anything, Gerty pushed a menu that she had collected from the table behind in Beth's hand.

Beth said, 'I'll have a jacket potato with coronation chicken and salad. For afters you can treat me to one of those cakes.'

She pointed to the selection of yummy delights in the cake cabinet on the far wall.

Beth asked Gerty, 'what you going to have?'

Gerty replied thoughtfully, 'I think I will have, uumm, the same as you. Yes the same.'

Gerty rose from the table and clambered through the cramped spaced tables to the bar where orders were taken and told the assistant what she wanted. She paid for it, got a ticket, and clambered back through to finally sit down and relax.

Gerty said, 'dam, I forgot the drinks.'

'Don't worry. When they bring the food, we will ask for them to fetch us some drinks.' Beth replied.

Gerty so relieved with that said, 'that sounds really good. '

Beth decided to go to the toilet. As Gerty looked around she noticed a napkin that was not there before in front of her. She picked it up and opened it. There was some writing. It read: YOU DEAD GERT!!!!! Gerty looked all around to see if she could catch a glimpse of who put the note there. Then she looked behind her to see who was close enough for them to have got so close to her in the first place. She then tried to remember who was sitting around and who had left suddenly. She found herself panicking. Gerty said to herself with her eyes closed for a moment. Now stop panicking. Whoever left the note is long gone. They did this to frighten me. Just stay perfectly calm. Then she thought, have I put my Mom in danger? Should we just go home? If we just go I would have to explain, just too much. Gerty decided to stay calm and carry on with her food and try to look and act as normal as possible. Beth came back from the toilet and the food arrived. Beth asked for two cups of tea. The waiter obliged.

Beth said, 'sorry Gerty did you want something else to drink?'

'No, that's fine.'

'Are you all right, you've gone white?'

'Yes, I'm fine. I thought I saw a ghost but it turned out to be nobody really.'

Gerty thought she covered that well. She felt the heat in her body rise with a blush.

For the rest of the shopping trip Gerty found her mind was elsewhere's. She bought a few Birthday presents and a few clothes for the boys. She bought some new books for the boys as well. She also bought a gift for Bella to say thanks for her support. It did not take away the fear of that napkin note. Gerty found herself on tender hooks, looking around every corner and face she came across. She was also wondering whether anybody was following them. She had a fabulous girlie time with her Mom shopping and appreciated the time spent with her. After her threat she realised how precious time could actually be. She dropped her Mom off and picked the boys up from school.

Again, months went by and it was business as usual. Gerty had almost forgotten the napkin threat and carried on as usual. Business was booming. Business was so good that Gerty thought about expanding but she would need more rooms and more space. She rented a house in the country side. The area was rural. It had farmer's fields for miles and one or two local residents. She thought Gerty's whorehouse, what a treat. It was not far from where Gerty lived. So, getting to and from Suldecote was easy. The tenant lived abroad. The only restrictions were to keep it looking respectable, clean and tidy. No wild parties, orgies and to not upset the neighbours. There was a private drive so nobody could see anything going on. Her clientele could come and go as they pleased.

THEIR NEW BUSINESS PREMISES

❦

The house had a Grand entrance. Two small pillars each side of the double doors. The hallway made a grand reception area for Bella to control and she was given an assistant. The assistant was a tall young thin blond woman/girl. She was a little dizzy with intelligence but she looked good. Her name was Wendy. The house itself had huge rooms that needed some TLC. It looked as if squatters had lived there for a short time. In one of the downstairs rooms was graffiti. She looked past the mess and dowdiness, which made the place a palace. She saw nooks and crannies of individualism caressed by originality and an overpowering scent of character. She knew instantly that this place would work for her fantasy world of pleasure and fun. Eight rooms needed special attention. They needed Gerty's artistic flair. The nearest and first two rooms were complete and ready for Carmen and Chelsea to do business. Gerty needed to interview a few more girls if she was to expand, she needed help. She asked her girls if they knew of anybody. Chelsea showed interest and said she would ask around. Bella just listened. Wendy was new to the business and knew nothing.

A month went by and the rest of the rooms were near to completion. A dark complexioned woman with black curly hair, slender body, and greeny blue eyes turned up out of the blue looking to talk to the owner. Bella phoned Gerty and Gerty drove as quickly as she could over to see her. Gerty had a brand new office for this very occasion. Gerty invited her in and asked how she could help.

The woman said, 'I have been a prostitute for decades and was looking to join a new outfit as the old one would not let her expand herself to submission toys.'

'Where do you come from?'

'Africa, I was brought over here by some of your country men, bought and sold. I worked as a prostitute for about fifteen years. I managed to escape and found other work. Now I want change.'

'Your submission techniques' are they violent, hurtful, and dangerous?'

'No, not at all. It is simply played as a game for whatever they want. It can hurt the nipples a little but not harmful.'

Gerty said as she leaned forward over the desk, 'I'm interested. When can you start?'

The woman said, 'right now. I have some equipment in my car.' Gerty said, 'I will show you to your work room.'

The room Gerty chose for her was painted a pale orange, tinted with yellow. There were flowers in a vase on an occasional table and pot plants scattered for decoration. You need to keep this room tidy at all times and it is your responsibility to look after the pot plants. If they die, it is your job to replace them.

'I have to go but sort out your hours of work with Bella downstairs. Any questions, ask Bella. What is your name?'

The woman replied, 'call me Cara.'

Gerty went downstairs to Bella and said, 'the ladies name is Cara. Be nice. No biting. I need to sort out a few things and will be back tonight.'

'Me bite if she nasty or rial me. If she good I be good.'

'Just keep the place running smoothly.'

With that, she left. As she approached the car a woman came up to her. She was tanned, had long ginger hair, brown eyes and you could not really see her shape because she had a padded coat on.

She walked over to Gerty and said, 'I hear you have some good clientele that need good workers?'

'Yes, as a matter of fact I do. Why, are you interested?'

The woman was of average height and spoke with an accent.

Gerty enquired, 'are you Polish or . . . . ?'

The woman replied, 'how did you know?'

'Your accent. You are not from around here. It was a lucky guess. Look, do you want to come in? I will show you around.'

'Yes please. I want a job, a permanent, fulltime job and I want to live in.'

'I have to go but I will leave you in the capable hands of Bella. What's your name?'

The woman thought for a moment and replied, 'its Trudy. My name is Trudy.'

Gerty said while they were walking into the house, 'how did you find out about this place?'

Trudy said, 'a friend told me.'

Gerty carried on asking, 'what is your story?'

Trudy said, 'excuse me?'

Gerty replied, 'your story, you know, how come you are a prostitute?'

Trudy said, 'I came from Poland and paid my way through working my body. Habits die-hard and I have no other qualifications and never been to school.'

Gerty replied, 'in this job it's not brains they want, is it?'

They reached Bella's reception and Gerty explained to Bella to settle Trudy into their business. She also told Bella to give her the low down on the rules.

Gerty had a quick word with Bella on her own, 'Trudy wants to be a resident.'

Bella glared at Gerty and said, 'no, here. We is strictly business premises. I close and lock me doors at ten dis night.'

Gerty said, quietly, 'you need to get one of the keys cut because she has nowhere else to go.'

Bella grunted, 'leave it all ta me, why don't ya?'

Gerty whispered, 'Bella, just listen. I have got no choice I have got other pressing engagements that can't wait. I will be back tomorrow morning.'

'I need to tark t ya about somting.'

'Oh and before I forget. The rooms in the basement?'

'Wat dose dirty, spida infested, filty dungeons. I would not put a dog down der. Wat ya want woman?'

'Cara needs some special equipment and those rooms need to become available for Cara to make it her pleasure dome. See to it and we will fit the bill.'

'Wat, ya crazy woman. It gonna cost a smart bitta cash girl.'

'I think she will turn it into a brilliant gold mine for us, Bella. Gotta fly, byeeeee. Talk to me tomorrow.'

Gerty flew out the door knowing she was running out of time for her bank manager's appointment.

When Gerty arrived she went straight into the bank manager's office. She knew him as one of her clients and they had a very amicable arrangement. He kept a certain amount of the profits with a free blow job occasionally with whom he wanted his pleasure with. Knowing Gerty had just employed two newbie's, he was ecstatic about her business plans for expansion. All the finances were passed as good and Gerty invited him over to have a look at the premises with some personal touches thrown in. Gerty worked all she could to get what she wanted.

The next day was all about settling in the newbie's and making sure the premises were in tiptop condition for her clients. She also had to inform old clients as well as new ones where she was, even if they already knew. A nudge in the right direction wouldn't do any harm. She spent most of the morning talking to her clients and also asking them if they knew of anybody else that needed her services. Bella did the same.

When they had finished Bella discussed Cara's work and told Gerty she never stopped last night. Cara's clientele list was growing rapidly.

Gerty said, 'they must like what she is doing then.'

Bella carried on by discussing Trudy, 'She likes her new room and told me she need to rest last night, cos she got clients booked in for later today.'

Gerty went back to her office. There was a card on her desk it read:

YOU ARE DEAD

GERT!!!!!!!!!

Gerty ran out of her office and grabbed Bella by the shoulder with the note in her hand.

She held it up to Bella's face terrified said, 'look, look.'

Bella took the card off Gerty and could not believe what she was looking at, 'dis is a det tret. Sombady want you cold lady.'

Gerty looked all around and asked, 'did you see anybody? Anybody that you didn't recognize or something unusual? Did you notice anybody strange hanging around?'

'Well, hell no. I seed nuffin. Everyting narmal here, girl.'

She let go of Bella's shoulder and Bella gave her a cuddle and said, 'I will step up der CCTV cameras and meke sure we got security in pleace in der right pleaces.'

Gerty smiled a terrified grin and walked back to her office. Gerty's mind was racing. She was having a panic attack. She poured herself a stiff whisky and threw herself into her chair. She gulped her drink and turned her classy-wheeled chair towards the window bay. She thought maybe they could have got in by the windows but none were open. She thought of her family and phoned. Her Mom answered but she did not say a thing.

'Mom, Mom say something . . . . Are you there?.'

Beth then replied, 'Gerty, what are you doing phoning at this time of the day? I thought you were working.'

'I am. I just thought I would phone and make sure you're alright.'

Beth, puzzled said, 'of course we're alright. Gerty what's going on?'

Gerty with a little light heartedness enquired, 'I can phone you can't I? Got to go Mom, I have work to do. Bye. Talk to you later when I pick up the boys.'

Gerty still couldn't focus and decided to walk the grounds that she had never done before. Nobody was about and Gerty started thinking about how serious her security really was. She stood at reception looking around every door, dark areas, stairs, and the entrance. She came to the conclusion anybody could just walk in and go to anywhere on the premises. Thinking about the obvious that just happened not long ago. It only took a few minutes to plonk that note on her table. After intensely engrossing in the challenges ahead she carried on her quest outside. Inch by inch she analyzed the building from a burglar's perspective, well, trying anyway. After going round from one side to the other she noticed the garden trees hid many possibilities for trouble makers to cause problems for her and her staff. She also thought after all everyone on the grounds is her responsibility. Before she only had to think about stairs, entry and exit. The six bedrooms and the reception area. Now she had a mammoth task ahead of her. Gerty realised she would have to spend money on security and call in the professionals. With that thought she went straight into her office and phoned a few companies for their input.

Gerty's day was so heavy. She picked up the boys from her Mom's did her usual Mother stuff and climbed into bed. The next day was another long and heavy day. This went on for about two months. At the end of it, all was well. The business was thriving. The front of the building had been changed so that access was controlled, safety and security was in place. Gerty started to feel a little safer.

JOE'S FINGER IS MISSING

Cara's toyshop was so popular that Gerty helped and made another room for its purpose. Chelsea was plodding along. The really new girl, Trudy was amazing. She worked fast and pleased the punters with her talents. She also worked long hours. Bella told Gerty that she had a word with Trudy to slow down and not to work so many hours.

Bella said, 'at the end of the day it's her choice.'

Gerty said, 'at the end of the day it's my business and I don't want her health to suffer. That reminds me, when do we get our checkups done?'

Bella replied whilst scouring her diary, 'in two wicks time. Mondey de fourt.'

The school phoned Gerty while she was talking to Bella in reception and said that they couldn't talk over the phone but she needed to come to the school right away. Gerty put the phone down, told Bella she was going to Joe's school and fled. She jumped in her car and sped the short distance to the school car park. She had to go to reception to tell them who she was and what she was there for. She was so angry that all this information was wasting precious time and she wanted to know what the problem was. She waited it seemed like forever for the Head Teacher to show her into her office.

She invited Gerty to sit down but Gerty was so wound up she said, 'just tell me. Is it Joe, has something happened to Joe?'

The Head teacher ordered Gerty to sit down and to try to stay calm. That was nigh on impossible. Gerty sat on the edge of the seat and looked wantingly at the Teacher.

The Head Teacher said, 'Joe has lost a finger.'

'What do you mean, lost a finger?'

The Head Teacher said, 'Joe told us a man, a tall man asked him to go over to the fencing because he had something for him. We tell them never to talk to strangers and not go by the fence but he did.'

Gerty said, 'yes, and?'

The Head Teacher continued, 'When Joe held out his hand the man grabbed his hand and cut off the little finger of his right hand.

Gerty shouted, 'what? Where's his finger now?'

The Head Teacher replied,' we don't know. We searched everywhere. The man must have taken it with him. The police have been called and they would like Joe and you to talk to them.'

Gerty panicked because of her work and said, 'I don't want to talk to no Police and neither does Joe. Where is he? I want to take him home?'

The Head Teacher replied, 'I'm afraid the Police want to question Joe about the man because it is a criminal offence. I don't think you have much choice and social services have to be called in. It's not just for Joe but the other pupils in the school. It could happen to them.'

Gerty angrily replied, 'all right, all right, where are the police? When are social Services coming then?'

The Head Teacher said, 'they had to go but if you would like to wait, they will be back shortly?'

'All right, we'll wait. Now can I see my son?'

By this time, Gerty was crying, in fact sobbing. Tears had smudged her makeup. The Head Teacher said that one of the teachers had taken him to the Jeff Enis Memorial hospital.

Gerty did no more than to rush out of the office, through reception, into her car and off to the hospital. When she arrived at the Hospital reception area she asked what ward was her son in. They checked on the computer and told her he was in casualty. Gerty knew the way and rushed there straight away. At A&E reception, she told them who she was and wanted to see her son. They showed her to a cubicle in casualty and a teacher confronted her.

Mr Poldark looked alarmed and said, 'the Doctor will be in shortly. I will leave you to it and wait in reception.'

With that, he walked off. Joe, with tears gushing, was so happy to see his Mom and got up to give her a cuddle. Gerty reciprocated. Gerty looked at his hand and saw a bandage full of blood.

She called the nurse, 'Nurse, Nurse, he's bleeding to death here.'

A Japanese Nurse came over and looked at Gerty.

She replied, 'the Doctor knows he's here. He won't be long.'

She could see more tears in Joe's eyes and when he spoke his lips trembled, 'Mom, he cut my finger off.'

He held his arm up towards her face and told her, 'it hurts.'

Just at that moment, the Doctor walked into the cubicle. He was a pot bellied, short, stout looking Indian with a strong London accent. He asked Joe what had happened and at the same time looked at his wound. He told Gerty and Joe that he needed to have surgery on his finger straight away. Gerty said nothing. She just listened. When the Doctor had finished a nurse came with a wheel chair and Joe sat in it. Gerty was told to follow the yellow lines on the floor until she reached a lift. She was to go up to the first floor and book Joe into the ward. The staff there would take it from there. Within an hour, Joe was taken to theatre but he was not put to sleep. The nurse told Gerty that they needed to close the wound as soon as possible and therefore Joe needed surgery right away. The big problem was they needed to do it right away and could not put him to sleep. Joe was given some sedation medication and his arm was injected with a numbing fluid. This meant that he would stay calm in the theatre and would not feel a thing. Within an hour, he was out of theatre and being wheeled onto the ward by Gerty. The nurse showed them his bed for Joe to rest and went off to deal with another patient. After an hour, the medication wore off and Joe asked if he could go and get something to eat.

The nurse said, 'yes but do not stay away too long. You need rest.'

The receptionist disappeared. There was no one around.

Gerty said, 'come on, we need to go home.'

Joe replied, 'we need to talk to the Police.'

'They will come round our house later.'

'Alright, I just need to get my bag from school.'

Gerty said agitated, 'we can pick it up tomorrow.'

With that, they both walked out of the building and got into the car.

They arrived home safely and Gerty told Joe, 'just to sit quietly while I do some stuff upstairs.'

She got all their suitcases down and filled them full of clothes and toiletries and anything else she could think of. She struggled downstairs but managed to put them all, including hers in the lounge.

Joe said, 'what you doin?'

'We are going on holiday.'

Joe said quizzically, 'where?'

'Uuummmmmmmm, don't know yet but on holiday all the same.'

Joe said, 'what about John? He's at Grandma's.'

Gerty could only think about getting away and forgot about John.

Thinking quickly, Gerty said, 'we are going to pick him up and then to the airport.'

Joe moaned, 'my whole arm is stinging. Have you got any pain killers?'

Gerty replied, 'Grandma will have some.'

Gerty's head was like a terrifying thought rush. She tried to think of everything all at the same time but found she was forgetting important bits like her son John. Suddenly she thought of her parents and she felt like a headless chicken that was going around in circles but not really achieving very much. She needed to tell someone about what was going on. In fact someone needed to tell Gerty what was going on as well, because she hadn't a clue. All she really knew was that she was putting other people's lives in danger because of something she didn't know. Her family was at risk. She opened the front door and put all the suitcases in the boot. She suddenly thought, the neighbours might be watching her. Dam, too late if they saw her they would have seen her put some suitcases in the back of the car. She then thought she had no time for paranoia. She swiftly turned round and called Joe to the car, strapped him into the front seat and checked that the house was all locked up and that the heating was off. She finally sat in the car. As she sat there she suddenly realised she had forgotten her hand bag and went back yet again into the house and picked it up from the settee. She decided that if she hadn't got what she needed she would buy it. The traffic was heavy outside her door and she waited for ever for a gap in the congestion but it came along all the same.

After about ten minutes she arrived at her parents' house. It was a semi-detached house with a small garage attached on the right. Beth, her Mom, liked pretty, dainty things like embroidered table clothes, crinoline Ladies and net curtains. She pulled up behind her Dad's old Escort, painted bright red. Joe slowly dragged himself out of the car. Beth saw them pull up and opened the door. Joe stood there with his arm in front of him and showed Grandma his huge bandage.

Beth said, 'Joe, what happened, what have you done?'

Gerty raced through and told her Mom she needed to talk to her in private. They both walked into the kitchen. Gerty said high to John as she walked past. Her father was in the kitchen having a cuppa. He looked at Gerty and could see how stressed she was.

Her Dad said, 'what's up girl?'

Gerty closed the door to the kitchen and started telling them the whole story. By the time she had finished her Mom was upstairs packing and her Dad was trying to find their passports. Gerty was in tears.

Gerty's Dad turned to her and said, 'where we going? Gerty replied where do you want to go? I thought Goa or Mauritius. They're supposed to be hot this time of year. Any ideas?'

Her Dad said, 'that sounds good.'

Beth put the suitcases in the old escort boot. She then came into the kitchen where Gerty and her husband were.

She said, 'Trevor, have you checked the water is turned off and the heating?'

Trevor replied, 'no, I'd better do it now.'

After making sure the house was secure, they all departed in their cars to Birmingham airport. Luckily, for Gerty their passports were new, as they had not long come back from a Turkish holiday with the boys.

FLYING HIGH TO SAFETY

———◆———

They arrived at the airport and parked both cars in the long stay car park. While they were getting the luggage out, the boys ran over and got some trolleys for the suitcases. They all walked over to the entrance of the airport. Gerty asked for everyone's passport and went to the booking in desk. They told her to get some tickets from another counter which she was directed to. She bought all the tickets to Mauritius and was told the next plane would arrive in five hours. They had no choice and they were lucky enough to get on any plane because they were usually pre-booked flights. Gerty asked if anybody was hungry and only the boys were. Gerty treated them to a Burger King feast. Later they sat in a lounge area and Gerty bought alcohol drinks for her Mom and Dad, plus one for her.

Bella phoned while they sat waiting.

Gerty said to Bella, 'I will be away for a couple of weeks. You're in charge of everything.'

'Wat ya do meeen. I can't run dis pleace on mi own.'

'Bella you're gonna have to. I have to get away, it's family.'

Bella barked, 'dis is yer bizniss. Yer responsibility is ere.'

The phone went dead. Gerty tried phoning back with no success. Gerty text instead.

She wrote: If I make you manager will you help???

Bella typed back: If I accept will ya give me a massive raise???????

Gerty typed back: Yes.

Bella typed back: tanx girl.

Gerty was so relieved that Bella was now in charge of her business. That meant that she could concentrate on her family and not worry.

After more than thirteen hours flying, they landed in Mauritius. Instantly they breathed a warmer, heavy and strange smelling breeze. It was not a nasty smell, just an almost dry, humid, and heavily fragrant with a touch of sulphur aroma. They were new to this environment. They got on the extremely long double bendy bus. It took them to where their luggage was being unloaded onto the carousel. Their job was to catch their luggage when they saw it, which was not as easy as they thought. Trevor spotted one of the suitcases and quietly mimed to Gerty that it was coming round her way. The idea was for her to catch it her end. She didn't but a gentleman standing next to her did for her.

As he passed it to her, she looked into his eyes and said, 'thank you.'

His wife had just got there's on a special trolley for the occasion and was demanding that the man go with her. Two boys about the same age as John and Joe followed them. He was a good looking man with blue eyes, huge pecks with shoulders to match and slenderly dressed with a white shirt and grey chino trousers. His bottom was firm and swayed to Gerty's liking. She found it difficult to take her eyes off his all.

The suitcases after that were collected in various ways but collected they were. They all walked towards the exit, went past security, and out into the coach filled car park. In the distance, she saw that man again and he walked towards a woman holding a sign that said, welcome to Mauritius Lilly Palace Hotel. Mauritian men of all shapes and sizes rushed over to help Gerty's family with their luggage. Many had already gotten a trolley for their convenience and the men to boys hustled for the grabbing of the suitcases. A young man of about eighteen won the heavy cases and heaved them onto his trolley. Next they called a taxi and the young man with all their cases followed them to the car. The taxi driver put some of the suitcases in the car and told Gerty that they would have to have another taxi as he would not get them all in his one. Gerty agreed and the man called another taxi to park behind him. The taxi driver said something in local dialect to the trolley boy and he pushed the rest of the suitcases to the taxi parked behind. Gerty and the boys got in the first one, Beth and Trevor got in the second. Gerty went to get into her taxi and the young boy got her attention by handing out his hand for payment for helping them. The taxi driver said you have to pay him for his services. She gave him two English pound coins and got into the taxi.

The taxi driver said, 'where would you like to go?'

Gerty replied, thinking about her new admirer, 'The Lilly Palace Hotel.'

The taxi driver carried on with, 'yes Ma'am. The trolley helpers prefer English money because of the exchange rate.'

'There are so many of them. Do they belong to the airport?'

The taxi driver said, 'no, but they do a good service. Not only that it is very difficult to get work on the Island and so that's why there are so many. They all have families to look after.'

Gerty's boys were so excited, even Joe with his fingerless hand had forgotten the pain and moved onto asking about where, what and why. Gerty answered some but not all questions. She didn't want the boys to worry, especially Joe; he had been through enough already.

Mauritius was a rundown wilderness. The houses were structures that needed advice from a health and safety aspect. You could see the locals were very poor with the kind of old, dirty and ripped clothing they wore. There was a big difference between working clothes and family stay at home clothes. Some of the roads needed repair and mostly none had paths at the sides. People walked on the roads carrying heavy bundles of goods. As they travelled they could see forests of lush green trees and bushes. There were streams thin and wide meandering through the country side. There were buildings half finished or half demolished, either way they were not finished. The people didn't look sad or unhappy. They just looked busy. Maybe they didn't know any better. Maybe they didn't have a choice.

The taxi driver pulled up outside the Lilly Palace and Gerty spoke in English to the guard. She had to explain that she had not booked anything but she wanted rooms for three adults and two children. The guard got on the phone and a car with two men came to talk to Gerty.

The men pulled Gerty over to the other side of the road and said, 'passport?'

Gerty gave them all the passports and told them she wanted two double rooms and two single beds with one room. She also explained that the stay would be initially two weeks but could be longer. Gerty hadn't a clue what type of hotel it was or where they were.

The guards said to Gerty, 'wait here. We have to check.'

They took the passports with them. The taxi driver was waiting but started to get impatient and eventually told Gerty that he had other people to pick up. Gerty's suitcases were taken out of the taxi and lent at the side of the guard house. The same with Beth and Trevor's luggage.

It was over an hour before the men came back. They were followed by two golf buggies.

The one man came over to Gerty and said, 'reception have your passports which is usual for them to keep them for a few days. There were only a few rooms available and the buggies will take you to them. Ma'am, you need to pay for the rooms first, so would you come with us and the buggies will take your family to their rooms?'

Gerty obliged.

When she got to the entrance she found herself in a beautiful Hotel. It really was a palace. The entrance doors were huge and made of carved wood. There were a few tiny steps to the doors and when you stood in the entrance, there was a reception area that opened out to other reception partitions and on the right, you could see a patisserie full of cakes and the smell of freshly ground coffee. In the far right hand corner there was a veranda and the ocean. Some waiters had trays of drinks serving people on the terrace. In front of the door was a huge reception table with the biggest bunch of Lilies on display. The floor was of shiny natural brownish marble. It shone so immaculately and Gerty worried she would slip or mark the floor walking on it. The men asked her to go to the main reception to her left. A lovely short Mauritian woman dealt with Gerty. She paid an extortionate amount of money for her rooms but they gave her the best rooms they had which was the Gold Star suite. Her parents had similar and the boys were next door with adjoining doors to Gerty's room. Gerty also paid for all inclusive to make life so much easier and she ate in the premiere dining areas. Gerty thought to hell with the expense for once. We are going to live a little. After all the checking, signing and discussions Gerty was shown to her room. They passed through the Hotel and the porter explained she could eat and drink at any of the restaurants on the premises. She was also told about towels for the beach, which were handed out at the towel reception area not far from the swimming pool bar. All this made Gerty really forget her problems and for the first time for days, totally relax.

The porter walked her down the stairs. She stood on the top step, mouth open. The view from where she was standing was designer. She had a full on view of the Indian ocean with Catamarans, sailing boats, people racing on jet skies, scuba divers and just underneath her outlook was a deep light blue swimming pool with people swimming or floating in it.

The Porter got her attention by saying, 'this way Ma'am.'

Everywhere she looked there were plants in flower, exotic, smelly Jasmine that wafted through the restaurant. The chequered ceiling beams housed other flowered plants. The restaurant was immaculate and laid out to an extremely high standard. The staff were getting ready for the lunch time session. This restaurant was a help yourself affair with everything on display. They carried on walking across, through and down to the gardens. In between bushes and especially built partitions there were bars, BBQ areas with restaurant seating. Another swimming pool that was not instantly visible and you could see that a bridge went under the large bar that lead to the beach. In front of that bar was white sandy beaches and a shallow wall made from local boulders. In front of the wall was a jetty with a built in landing fifty pence hexagon shaped building with no sides, just a roof.

She walked on past the hairdressers onto a path that you could see on the left of the hotel guest rooms. The palm trees and grassland were set in about an acre of gardens. On the right was the ocean in multi coloured blues, greens and browns. You could also see what looked like rocks in the water, it was so clear. Again on the right was a small stream that ran from under the hotel guest rooms. They crossed over a tiny bridge and Gerty stopped to have a look at the beauty that was surrounding her. She heard birds in the trees and saw different coloured shaped and sized fish. The sandy bottom was a little duller, greyish brown sand but beautiful all the same.

The Porter looked back and smiled at Gerty, 'not far now Ma'am.'

With that, Gerty carried on following him. She looked on her right and saw the seductive man at the airport who helped her with her luggage. He had just come out of the cool water and was dripping wet. Gerty melted when she saw his near naked body. She walked slowly and eventually caught his eye. His wife was sunbathing with her eyes closed and their boys were having fun at the water's edge. She smiled at him flirtishly and walked on. He smiled back intrigued, wanting to know more. His eyes never left her until she disappeared around the corner of the building.

The Porter said, 'here Ma'am just up to the top and you are there.'

Gerty asked, 'did we take the long route round then?'

The Porter replied, 'yes Ma'am but it was to show you around at the same time. If we kept on walking instead of turning left there is your special restaurant.'

Gerty asked quizzically, 'what do you mean our special restaurant. I thought we could go to any of them?'

The Porter was still climbing the stairs with Gerty by his side and answered, 'yes Ma'am, that is perfectly true but you have extra privileges and can eat where you want. That restaurant that I pointed out is your own restaurant, shared by others of your standard, Ma'am.'

Gerty thought, wow my standard it must be good. She smiled a cheeky smile at the Porter as they arrived at the door of her rooms.

A swipe card opened the door. She was asked that if she went off the premises to hand the key into reception for safekeeping. She was in heaven when she saw the design. It was palatial, classy and seductive all at once. The porter put her luggage down by the bed and walked over to a built in cabinet.

He opened it and said in his sales pitch, 'the fridge is for your convenience. Help yourself to whatever you want. It is checked every day and you will get your bill for what you have consumed at the end of your stay.'

He closed the fridge and walked over to a door in the corner. Gerty followed. They both looked in but Gerty just carried on looking. She was fascinated by the decor. It was just so gorgeous.

The Porter went into automatic and said, 'the shower is a walk-in wet room with, soap, shampoo, tooth paste, a cap for your hair and the hair dryer is over there away from the water. Everything is replaced if you use it for your convenience and the towels are changed every day.'

He came out of the bathroom and over to the mirrored desk.

He said as he picked up a brochure and some leaflets, 'if you want room service all telephone reception numbers are in this booklet. If you want some excitement these leaflets will explain some excursions for your pleasure. One last thing if you want food, in that booklet there is the number of the restaurants, if they have got it they will make something up or choose from the menu which is at the back of the booklet.'

'I bet you're worn out after all that.'

The porter replied, 'I am, yes. If you would like anything else just phone or ask at reception.'

Gerty leaned on the bed and got her purse out of her handbag. She opened it and gave him some English coins. They were mostly two pound and pound coins.

She put a handful in his hand and said, 'thank you for all your help.'

The Porter was impressed with English money because he knew he could get a good return for them, when the time was right. The Porter left the room quietly. Gerty took a deep sigh of relief, slumped on the bed, and looked at the ceiling for a minute or two. She heard some noise coming from the next room and realised it was the voice of her sons. She got up and walked to a door that looked like a partition door. It must lead into the next room she thought. It had a key in it and she turned it, opened it, and saw her two rascals jumping, pillow fighting on the single beds provided. Joe jumped down as if he had done nothing wrong. John on the other hand was in mid air and was just about to fling his pillow at Joe. Too late he did what he intended and Gerty walked forward. John stumbled off the bed as he noticed it was his mother.

Gerty smiled and uttered, 'I have had an idea. Why don't we go down to the beach?' The boys just kept saying, 'yes, yes, yes.'

Gerty told them to get changed quickly and she would be back in a minute. Gerty went out their apartment door to the next-door and knocked. Beth answered and she invited Gerty in.

Trevor said, 'wow, this is posh. In fact it's gorgeous.'

Gerty said, 'is everything all right?'

Trevor came over and gave Gerty a cuddle.

'How long have we got?'

'I've booked us in for two weeks.'

Trevor said smiling, 'noooo, how long before we all go down to the beach? We heard you ask the boys. These walls are like paper.'

Gerty replied with an even bigger smile, 'that's what I've come to ask. Would you like to come down to the beach with us?'

Trevor replied as he showed off his trunks under his trousers, 'I'm ready.'

Beth by this time had moved over to the window and taking in the designer view.

Trevor asked, 'will we need towels?'

Gerty said, 'apparently not. They have a towel reception here, which is situated by the left side of the swimming pool and not far from the beach.'

Trevor said, 'come on Beth, have you got a swimming costume?'

Beth tersely replied, 'I'm all right as I am thanks.'

She picked her handbag up from the chair and looked at Gerty with a blank expression, 'shall we go?'

Gerty quietly replied, 'yes, I'll go get the boys and my costume.'

With that, Gerty walked out the door, through the boy's room and to her apartment, she picked up her costume and stuffed it in her handbag that was almost big enough to be a suitcase. She went to the boy's room and they marched to Grandma's and Granddad's room. The door was open and Gerty's parents were just coming out. Beth had the key disc in her hand and she closed the door. It was strange not having bulky towels to cart with them.

After walking down three flights of stairs they reached the bottom. There were some stray dogs in the distance that looked quite healthy. Gerty thought the restaurant staff were looking after them or the guests were feeding them. They all followed the path around to the scenic view of the building and saw the breath taking view of the ocean. The boys ran all the way. Stripped their day clothes off, left them in a pile on the sand, and ran to the shore with their swimming costumes on. Trevor smiled with Gerty, watching the boys having such an exciting time.

Gerty suddenly realised and shouted, 'Joe, Joe, don't get your bandage wet.'

Trevor said with a worried smile, 'whoops, too late.'

Gerty ran to where Joe was and analysed his bandage. It was dripping.

Gerty said in her, I give up tone, 'Arrh well, just go have some fun, Joe.'

Joe said worryingly, 'sorry Mom.'

Gerty kissed him on his head and said, 'worse things have happened at sea, boy. Off with you.'

Joe smiled and ran back to John with a kick splash in his face. John reciprocated. Trevor and Beth reached the sand. Trevor walked over to some sun beds and called Beth over to sit on one next to him. She obliged and sat but with a heavy heart and expression.

Beth said to Trevor, 'has Gerty brought this on herself, I wonder?'

Trevor replied, 'even if she has, that gives nobody reason to cut a boys finger off.'

Beth said, 'thinking about it she was being threatened well before the Joe incident.'

Trevor replied, 'she has obviously stepped on some bodies toes but she doesn't even know what it's all about.'

Beth said worryingly, 'it's very worrying and could affect all of us.'

With that thought in mind, Gerty came up to her deck chair and said, 'Mom, I know you think it's my fault that we're in this mess but I didn't ask for this. All I've been trying to do is make a living so I can give my boys a good upbringing.'

Beth growled, 'yes by doing a proper job without lying on your back.'

Gerty growled at her, 'Dad, Dad can you tell her it's my choice and I do it very well thank you and I earn a dam site more than I would do if I worked erect.'

Trevor was flabbergasted and looked at Beth. Beth got out a magazine that she bought at the airport and hid her face in it. Gerty stormed off and got changed by the boy's clothes and joined the boys by splashing them. They in return splashed back. After a few seconds Gerty and the boys were jovial.

Gerty spent the rest of the day playing, Beth spent it ignoring everybody and Trevor was an in between. He didn't want to rock the boat but he was quite a placid kind of guy. He did not approve of his daughters job but if that is what she wanted to do then providing she kept it to herself, he was all right about it. He just didn't want all the upset and falling out. He most certainly didn't want to play piggy in the middle of two women arguing. He felt this most unfair.

Tempers calmed as they all went back to the apartments and showered ready to dress for their evening meals.

SEDUCE ME PLEASE

The meals were exceptional and the variety amazing. The restaurant was a stone's throw away from the beach and the candles on the tables reflected in the ocean as the evening sky fell over the flat ocean. The colours looked to have been painted, blended and bled into each other. It didn't look real. There were so many colours in one sky and they flowed forever in each direction. Distant silhouettes of rolling hills and jagged tree tops set the scene.

Gerty's Mom was quiet and Trevor, tense. The boys had had a full on day and enquired about going to the shore for another dip of joy and frivolity. Gerty was tired and tried to make things work. She felt guilty and blamed herself for everything that had happened. The headless chicken had gone and the remorse set in. The best thing though, was that they had all the time to reflect, to calm, and let them blend into holiday mode for a while. Not a lot was said through the evening meal and even when they all went to their rooms, a quiet good night was murmured. All doors closed. Gerty put the boys to bed and threw herself onto her bed and had a sobbingly good cry. She was conscious of the boys being able to hear so she kept sobbing but from the balcony.

The light from her room caught the silhouette of her body underneath. Her dress was filled with the pattern of tiny multi-coloured chiffon on a black back ground. It was a floaty number that frilled at the hem in two layers. She looked gorgeous. She felt gorgeous but something was missing and she did not want to be on her own. She turned and walked to the fridge. Got herself a glass, a small bottle of Gin and a small can of lemon and tonic water. She then poured it in the glass from her veranda. She heard noises and thought it was coming from the next room on her left. The boys were on her right. She ignored it and carried on pouring. She heard it again but this time she heard somebody calling. She looked right and left and then over the balcony. There in front of her was the fella from the airport; the guy that helped her with her luggage.

She smiled and quietly said, 'hi, how are you?'

He replied, 'I'm good. Would you like to come for a walk?'

Gerty thought this was just the tonic she had hoped for. A man in her life. Somebody else's man she also acknowledged.

Then quickly thought, Arrh what the heck, he'll do.

She whispered 'hang on a minute.'

'I'll be down, just hold on.' He whispered, 'I'm hanging. I'm hanging.'

She met him by the steps at the back and he smiled with elation at her.

He asked, 'soooooo, what brings you to Mauritius?'

Gerty answered, 'we decided to have a quick holiday.'

'How long are you here for?'

'We have booked in for two weeks, you?'

'We're just here for the week.'

He grinned with his hormones and said, 'you look gorgeous in that dress. You look gorgeous anyway but that dress suits you.'

Gerty blushed and said, 'you're not so bad yourself.'

They walked to some of the beach chairs and sat and talked some more. It was mainly a questions and answers quiz. After about an hour or so, she got up and walked over to the beach wall that was higher, further away from the hotel. The lights had faded and the atmosphere was more seductive. She sat on the wall as he came close to her.

She quietly and seductively spoke, 'I would like to be seduced, but I don't like to ask.'

His eyes caught the light and his head bent down to her ear as his hands crawled around her tiny waist. Gerty spread her legs, one at each side of his thighs.

'I have wanted to hold you since the first time I saw you.' I would have pleasure in seducing you if you'd let me.'

They kissed and the rest was orgasmic history.

Gerty got what she wanted and she certainly dangled the carrot in the right direction. Next day was more fun and games with John and Joe on the beach but her new found toy was watching her every move whilst his Wife sunbathed oblivious to the chemistry between them. He was dripping with come and get me hormones and Gerty the same. She had to be careful though because she didn't want her Mom to see what was going on. Gerty turned her attention to the boys and played in the ocean. The day was relaxed and the evening too. The night came and so did the fun and frolics for her new found friend.

He came to the veranda and Gerty was dressed ready for the next sexual encounter but this time she had a business plan and he was the business. They walked on the beach flicking the sand with their toes.

'What would you say if I told you I was a working girl?'

'What if I told you I was a working man?'

Gerty became confused.

She embarrassingly questioned, 'I don't even know your name?'

He teasingly held her hand and carried on walking saying, 'what would you like to call me?'

Gerty smiled and replied, 'I think you could be (she analysed his face) a Sebastian.'

'Why a Sebastian?'

Gerty followed by saying, 'I like that name and it suits you.'

'Ok, my name is . . . . Sebastian.'

She cheekily glared at him, ignored his reply, and carried on, 'you could be a John, George, Alfred, or even a Matthew?'

'I am . . . . none of them.'

She put her arms around him from the front to his waist and gently rubbed his side.

Gerty softly said, 'are you a Jonathon Ross? I like him too.'

He gently spoke, 'my name really is Jonathan. Was that a guess or have you been checking up on me?'

Gerty kissed him passionately, then took a short breather and whispered, 'Jonathan . . . Ross.'

He pulled away and chuckled, 'You can't kiss me like that and call me Jonathon Ross.'

Gerty chuckled back and said, 'why not without the Ross we're almost there.'

He grabbed her close and squashed her into his hips.

'I want to give you more of me. Where can I do it?'

'I am a working girl and you will have to pay.'

He pulled her away, held her waist, and said quietly, 'you want me to pay you to have sex with? You're a, a prostitute?'

'And a bloody good one at that.'

His amorous temper was raising but his lust for her overwhelmed him. He also knew this was only going to be a holiday fling to entertain his loins. He also knew he didn't love her but craved her attention for his own gratification.

He looked her up and down and asked, 'how much?'

'In English money it would depend on what you wanted?'

Jonathon quickly answered all of it. Gerty's face lit up because she was after some fun too but more so company with sex thrown in.

Gerty asked softly as she stroked his hair back, 'what is everything?'

Jonathon excitedly said, 'I name the place and I choose what we do.'

Gerty replied softly and positively with a kiss on his cheek, we have to be discreet. We both have other people to think about.

He replied, 'I forgot to tell you discreet is my second name.'

She walked him over to a park bench behind some trees and softly, sexily, whipped off her thong and whispered as she pulled him on top of her, 'this one's for me. Caress my insides with your manly pleasures.'

He did what he was asked and more.

For the rest of the week he called on her most nights and once through the day. In fact, while they were both having lunch in the same restaurant. A sleazy place to have sex in the toilets, but it felt so good and they both wanted to feel like naughty children. He paid her well before he left and asked when she went back to Britain to let him know where she was and he would want to see her on a regular basis. She told him he would be sadly missed and her body would pine for him. He left wanting.

BELLA WANTS GERTY'S UNDIVIDED ATTENTION

———◆———

Gerty made a comfortable amount of money to be able to give her Mom and Dad spending money for the planned two weeks. The boys got pocket money if they behaved and spent their dosh on clothes or slot machines that were scattered around the Hotel. There was also a games room where they could play all sorts of table games but they had to pay. It did not seem a lot but it all added up to more than Gerty gave them. They persuaded Gerty to give a little extra occasionally.

Gerty got a phone call.

It was Bella, 'Gerty, ya com ome, now. I need ya ear wid me. Der is som tings I can't do wid out ya. I need ya ere to elp mi wid new peoples. Ya com ome, you ear?'

Gerty said, 'can't you deal with it. It is very difficult at the moment. I need time away for a couple of months.'

Bella screamed, 'I need ya ear lady. Ya git yer butt over ere or I leavin. You ear, leavin.'

Gerty suddenly panicked and said, 'I will be on the next flight home. Stay there and I will be there sometime tomorrow or the next. I need to find the next available flight. I am on my way. Bella, can you hear me? Bella, Bella.'

Bella was crying and replied, 'ya git back ear. You com back, ya ear?'

Gerty said, 'yes, just calm down. I will be back shortly.'

Gerty's Dad was on the beach with her.

She turned to him and said, 'Dad I have got to go back home but on my own. I need to go now will you hold the fort here. I will make sure you are all looked after while I am gone.'

Trevor said, 'we can't stay here forever and it must be costing you a fortune?'

Gerty beggingly replied, 'don't worry about the money side. We are safe here but will you look after Joe and John for me, please Dad?'

Trevor replied, 'yes, but what about their schooling and their friends? We can't go on forever like this?'

'Right, Dad leave it to me. Just answer me one question, would you like to live here?'

Trevor said, 'I haven't even thought about it.'

Gerty said, 'discuss a place to live outside the U.K. and we will go and live there. I certainly have the money and can buy abroad. I can't go back to the U.K. so our destiny is in your hands. Dad I have got to go. I have to catch a plane. I won't be long a week or so at most.'

Gerty went straight to reception and was able to book another two weeks for them to stop and at a lower rate than before. She also booked flight tickets through the receptionist for that night to fly back to England. The receptionist had already given their passports back and so Gerty was ready for the off. She didn't pack a thing. She just got in the ordered taxi and went straight to the airport. She waited about three hours for her flight, got on it and relaxed. The captain walked her way to stretch his legs and low and behold it was Jonathon. She couldn't believe her luck.

He leaned over her and asked whisperingly as if he were talking about her seat belt, 'have you ever joined the mile high club?'

Gerty softly said, 'no what's the mile high club?'

He softly said, 'come with me.'

She slipped the lock of the seat belt and walked in front of him down the aisle. The other staff was at the other end. He pulled the curtain too and pushed them both into the toilet room. He then managed to close the door.

Gerty said, 'there's not much room in here.'

He said, 'this is the mile high club room. Knickers down. It's my job to check that all passengers are healthily sorted.'

Gerty said, 'you can check my temperature any time providing you pay and this is gonna cost.'

'Oohh and I thought I was gonna get a free sample. Not to worry I will pay you when you are on the ground and the next time I see you.'

Gerty was pressed into position and her temperature taken. My, she found it hot, sweaty, and most exhilarating.

When they had finished playing, Jonathon said, 'I'll go out first to make sure the coast is clear.'

After a few moments, Gerty was pulled out of the clubroom. They walked down the aisle as if they didn't know each other. Gerty sat in her chair and belted up. The captain glanced back with a cheeky grin. Gerty thought phew he is so hot. I think I am falling in love with him. She day dreamed the rest of the journey and felt extremely safe. All her worries seemed to disappear. She didn't see Jonathon after the flight and was saddened by it. She was hoping for a tiny glimpse of her sex friend.

As she was carrying only her handbag, customs was just a walk through. Gerty found her car exactly where she had parked it and got the keys out of her handbag. She drove from the airport after paying her car-parking fee. The drive was just under an hour's journey from the airport. Bella was so relieved to see her that she cried on arrival. Bella knew she was coming but didn't know when.

Bella shuffled Gerty into Gerty's office and said, 'sid down girl, I will pour ya a stiff Gin and tonic.'

'Sounds nice.'

'You is gonna need it honey.'

'Why?'

Bella picked up a box from her desk and moved it closer on the desk to her.

Bella shivered and said, 'I know it's got yer neme on it, but it com from der flat we're we used to werk at and I needed to find out.'

Bella reiterated what she had said; 'it's got yer neme on it.'

Gerty suddenly felt a rush of horror. She also thought this can only get worse. Gerty leaned forward and pulled the flaps of the box. She could see blooded tissue paper. She lifted out of the box with pinched fingers so as not to get any fluid on her. As she lifted the blood drenched tissue paper out so too did a note come out. A piece of white typed A4 paper. It read in huge letters:

YOU ARE DEAD GERT!!!

The tissue had stuck to it something pinkish and as they pulled more, the pink thing fell on the floor and rolled under the chair. Gerty looked down and saw Joe's dead finger. It had been cut off from the top of the palm. The whole finger joint had been severed. Gerty dashed to the nearest place to be sick, which was the sink in the corner of her office.

Bella looked down and screamed, 'its somebadies TAJA (penis). Its bin cut off. Why?'

Gerty told her the whole sad story. Bella now understood the urgency of running away.

Bella asked bewildered, 'why? Who would do such a ting? Gerty why you?'

Gerty replied as bewildered as Bella with tears rolling down her face,' I just haven't got a clue.'

Bella was a gentle soul with a heart of gold for her friends and Gerty was her friend, whether she liked it or not. Bella also looked after Gerty whether she liked it or not. Bella's Mom was none too kind and did not help Bella bring up her kids very often. In fact Bella was treated as an inconvenient child that was brought up by her grandparents most of the time. Her mother had psychological problems through drugs. Her upbringing was very strained.

Bella went and made a cup of tea. Gerty just carried on crying in her office, she felt sorry for herself, also for putting Joe, John, her Mom, and Dad through the mill. Gerty was helpless with overwhelming emotion. Bella came into the room with a tray. On it was a teapot, some cups, cake, and biscuits. She put the tray on one of the side tables and played mother. She poured out the tea into a cup and saucer and plated some cake and biscuits for Gerty. Gerty sipped and picked at the food. She had lost her appetite.

The evening went quiet and her office turned into a room for thought. Bella had made herself available by putting her new assistant in charge of reception and so making it occupied at all times. She needed to talk business with Gerty but Gerty was in no frame of mind for anything. Bella told Gerty that she had made her bed up in her working room and that she was to stay in their while she was here. Gerty went to bed early and Bella went home to her kids.

Early next morning the mist lay suspended heavily on the lawns outside. It made the house look eerie. Bella arrived about eight thirty and took over the reception duties. Gail the receptionist went home.

Bella saw Gerty coming down the stairs. She was dressed and ready for business. Gerty had a dress on that she had left in her wardrobe. She also realised that she needed to get some more clothes for travelling back to Mauritius with. Gerty went into the dining room and met Cara, Chelsea and Trudy. They were all chatting away and it sounded like they all got on really well. Gerty walked in and the girls stood up.

Gerty said, 'nice to hear you all getting on so well and to hear you have all settled in well.'

Cara said, 'yes, has Bella had a word with you about expanding?'

All the ladies sat down and listened intently.

Gerty replied, 'I am having a meeting with Bella later this morning.'

As Gerty finished talking, Bella walked briskly into the room.

She turned to Gerty and said, 'right den are we ready?'

Gerty put some breakfast quickly on a large plate, held it in one hand and picked up her mug of tea she had made a couple of minutes earlier and replied, 'ummmm, well, yes Maaaaam.'

Gerty smiled at the other ladies and they all chuckled back.

Gerty sat in her office chair and Bella sat on one of the other ones by her desk. She was used to sitting in Gerty's chair and was getting used to being the Manager.

'There are going to be many changes to this business because it is growing fast.'

'Yes, I want to tark to ya about staff.'

Gerty was enthusiastic and said, 'what ideas have you got?'

Bella eagerly put her ideas on the table and said, 'I bin asked to interview dees prostitutes but I neva dun interviews befar.'

Gerty suggested, 'while I am here perhaps I could do that for you?'

Bella gratefully said, 'I would apreshiate dat.'

Bella carried on, 'I want anova receptionist so I can run der bizniz properly and I got a lady in mind fur dat.'

'Anybody I know?'

'No I don't tink sow. She can start right awey.'

Bella thought she might push a little harder and quickly asked, 'and could we have a cleaner, cos I can't do evry tink?'

Gerty butted in, 'and a maid.'

Bella looked overjoyed and said, 'can I? I mean can we?'

'I am putting my business in your hands for the time being. You must make it pay.'

'All right, I want to open der flat back up and git some more prostitutes in der. It worked fer us it can work agin. Dat means anuder receptionist to work like I did.'

'You have really thought this through and I am so proud of you Bella.'

Gerty went on to say, 'you need experience with interviewing. You can sit in on the ones I will do while I'm here.'

Bella nodded and said, 'all right.'

'We are forgetting one big detail.'

'What is dat?'

'We need more girls for the flat. In fact we need two more girls for the flat.'

'No worries Gerty. Me plan is to ask dee oder prostitutes to work der until we find more.'

'Good thinking Batman.'

'Right, plan of action. Ask Wendy to phone those ladies up and ask them to come for an interview as soon as they can.'

'What about your receptionist? Can you get her to start right away?'

'Ooooooooooh, dat bi Grand.'

'Is there anything else you want to talk to me about?'

'Yes, Cara is, you know, battin fer dee oder side.'

Gerty said carefully to Bella, 'I know our workers are prostitutes and their work is prostitution but could you call them workers or something else. Prostitute is such an ugly word. Maybe you could come up with another more pleasurable title for our hard working workers, perhaps.'

Bella chuckled and said, 'dey could arl bi known as Dirty Gerty's ladies or Madam's.'

Gerty chuckled as well and replied, 'you cheeky bitch.'

Gerty thought while she was there she would try to get to know the girls a little better. She went to the dining room and Cara was cooking up some kind of casserole.

Gerty sat down and asked Cara, 'I've been told you bat for the other side, is that right?'

'Yes that is why I like the weapons of dominance but I haven't got a partner. I am single, unattached and on my own, boo hoo hoo.'

Gerty smiled, 'me too but I don't bat for the other side. I like men too much.' 'How long have you been in the business?'

'I was fourteen when I started. My gorgeous boyfriend decided to sell my services to his friends. At that age I didn't know what was going on until one day I asked for some of the money I earnt and he told me to fuck off.

Fuck off is exactly what I did and fucked all his mates but kept the money. He was really pissed off and beat me up. Unfortunately for him, his friends did not like what he did to me and they broke both his legs. I still have one of his friends on my list of punters now.'

Cara was impressed and replied, 'good for you.'

Cara finished what she was doing and put the kettle on. She asked Gerty if she wanted a cuppa and Gerty responded with a yes.

Gerty went on to say, 'I love what I do and have achieved quite a bit.'

'This place is a gold mine. My books are full. Oh dam, I got to go. I've a punter at twelve and I got to get ready.'

'Gerty, can you turn that casserole off. It's for us all later.'

Gerty at this point needed a change of scenery and told Bella she was going shopping. Bella was very busy organising and so Gerty left her to it. She shopped till she dropped in Nuneaton town centre. They had a varied collection of clothes and Gerty was in a fashionable, different things to wear, kind of mood. She bought shoes, dresses. She adored dresses, especially floaty chiffon types that were see through in parts. She needed new sexy, come and get me under wear. The type you can't wait to get off from a man's point of view but all the same comfortable to wear. Nighties, the flowing type that you could just about hide whilst sitting in a chair but once stood you could see the most intimate parts of her curvaceous body parts. She also needed dressing gowns to match. Next she needed sexy, stunning attire for her work. She needed loads of different stockings and Basques. She also needed more sex toys and because of her profession and the sex industry, she was able to get some free samples. Suddenly she realised she was going back to Mauritius and desperately needed new swim wear. She bought about three or four gorgeous all in one suits with matching wraps and tops to strut her beautiful body on the beaches. It was quite difficult to get swim wear this time of the year but luckily some shops had the sense to just for her. Her last shop was back to the shoe shop. She wanted a couple of pairs of boots. Some for work and some to play but mostly to look good either way.

She arrived at her business and realised it hadn't got a name. The business needed a name. It was very late and she hadn't had anything to eat since morning. She was on a high and in a happy bubble.

When she entered the building, Bella looked back and said, 'ya add a good shoppin den?'

Gerty swung her bags around and danced up the first two steps.

She smiled, 'uumm yes, I have bought happiness and joy to us all. I have some free samples.'

'I will ave a look at dem leater. You know ya wanted to see dem new workers? Well dey is ear. Waitin for ya to git back. So when yer ready?'

Gerty retorted, 'what now?'

'Dats dee idea girl.'

Gerty retorted, 'what right this second, now?'

'I will bring one to yer office in five minutes.'

Gerty rushed with all her bags into her bedroom, plonked all on the bed and flew back down the stairs to her office.

She stood by her desk as Bella showed the two girls in.

'Could I see each of you individually please?'

'Dey is sisters and would prefer to be togeder.'

Gerty thought it strange but said, 'right, ok. Please take a seat and welcome to our world.'

Gerty observed that the one girl had a deep scar on her arm. She also noticed these too ladies were of Asian origin. Their skin was tanned and their long black hairs were platted in the traditional way but their attire was European. They wore jeans and tee-shirts. Gerty started by saying, 'tell me about yourselves then.'

The right hand lady started first. The one without the scar.

She said, 'my name is Rajinder and we are sisters. This is Harjinder. We both were used and abused by my father, relatives and friends when we were about nine years old. If we didn't perform my father would whip my mother, so we had no choice. Our father sold us to some Europeans when we were about ten and a half and we ended up in Birmingham, Soho.'

The other lady just kept on nodding to everything her sister said.

Gerty said to the other lady, 'why are you here? Why not come out of prostitution altogether?'

Both girls looked at each other and the girl on the left answered, 'we never had an education. We don't know anything else, just what we have been told to do.'

Rajinder butted in, 'we would like to join your house. We feel we have picked up many things that men would like us to do, especially both together. We have run away from those men that battered us and abused us so we can be free to do what we want to do without the pressure. We also worked long hours and many times seven days a week. We want to work but need our own space as well. Will you please give us a job, please?'

Gerty said, 'I have no problem giving you jobs. Sort the hours you want to work and where you want to work because we have flats in Warwick as well. Will you want your own rooms or would you prefer to work together?'

Harjinder replied, 'I would like my own privacy if that is acceptable?'

Gerty said, 'no problem.'

Gerty thought for a moment and said, 'is it possible to give you working names?'

Rajinder replied 'yes, but what?'

Gerty thought again, 'perhaps for you Rajinder, Crystal?'

Rajinder smiled and said that sounds very nice.

I will be known as Crystal.'

Rajinder asked, 'what about me?'

Gerty said, 'how about Charlie or Leila, maybe?'

Rajinder replied, 'I like the sound of Charlie.'

'Charlie it is then.'

Gerty, still sitting rang reception on her desk phone, which she did not do often.

Wendy answered, 'Hi Gerty, how can I help?'

Gerty surprised to hear Wendy's voice said, 'oh, hi Wendy, can you show these two ladies to their new rooms and fill in the paperwork?'

Wendy replied, 'yes, no problem. Will there be anything else?'

Gerty was again surprised by Wendy's professionalism and asked if the other ladies of the house could show the ladies around when they have got a minute?

'Yes, no problem.'

'That's all for now, Wendy,' and put the phone down.

The women went to stand up.

Gerty said, 'I think, if you escaped you did so with the clothes you have on. Here is my credit card. Do not go over the top but do buy yourself a wardrobe for work and a wardrobe for yourselves. Don't forget undies and beautiful shoes, boots and slippers perhaps. Anyway, it's up to you but be practical, sensible and I want you pair looking gorgeous.'

The women did not know what to say and quietly whispered thank you with tears in their eyes.

'Just keep your receipts and give them to Bella. They can go on the business account.'

The ladies stood up with Gerty following them to reception. Wendy walked round from the reception desk and asked the ladies to follow her with a welcoming smile. Gerty was very, very impressed.

Gerty turned and told Bella she was going upstairs to enjoy the rest of her day.

'See Bella, interviewing can be very straight forward. Next time you will do the interviews and I will just watch. Does that sound good?'

'Tanx Gerty.' Dat be brilliant.'

Gerty, after a few minutes went upstairs herself. She walked into her room and started looking at all the presents, clothes, shoes and unpacked each and every one of them. She now had time to try them on. One by one shoes to dress was worn and matched then hung in the wardrobe until all had been thoroughly inspected again. She revelled in the excitement of new things. Cara knocked on the door just as Gerty had finished with a bowl of her casserole in hand.

Cara said, 'I will leave you with this. I know you haven't eaten much today and you have been very busy.'

'Thanks Cara, you're right, I'm starving.'

With that, Cara went back down stairs. Gerty put the bowl down on a side table, put the bags away and with bowl in hand again sat on the side of her bed. The smell was so moreish and the colours of the vegetables made it look mouth watering. She took a sip and a bite. The flavours melted into heavenly warmth in her mouth.

TIME TO CHANGE LIVES

———❦———

Next morning Gerty knew she did not have much time left and had to get back to her family in Mauritius. Bella found Gerty and introduced her to Mushka.

Mushka said, 'you don't remember me do you?'

Gerty quizzically replied, 'should I?'

Bella said, 'Mushka used to work for you at the old flat, many years ago.'

Gerty looked intently at her face and complimented her, 'blimey you've got younger.'

'I remember now. You had seven kids and a very good husband. How are you doing?'

'The husband lost his job and can't find work, so he asked me if I wanted to go out to work and he be the house husband. He was joking but I was not. That is why I'm here. Bella tells me you want another receptionist come assistant for the old flat?'

Gerty said, 'yes we are opening it up again. Bella's idea this time. When can you start?'

Bella said, 'she is startin reet dis minute. I is tekin her over to der flat now.'

Gerty looked at Mushka and said, 'nothing's changed, I still get told nothing.'

Mushka said, 'we must get together and catch up.'

'After I come back from Mauritius we will do that, definitely Mushka.'

Gerty quickly said, 'Bella, while I remember, I need a flight back to Mauritius and a taxi to the Lilly Palace Hotel when I get there. Can you arrange that for me please?'

'No problem. I will git Wendy on it reet awey.'

Gerty thought she needed to check on their houses to see that nobody had burnt them down while they had been away. That was her next port of call.

The rain came down in buckets outside her Mom's house and the house looked alright. She did notice two stockily built men in a car just down the road that looked to be guarding the house. Gerty went in and the bully boys were sitting outside the house. Gerty thought how the hell am I going to get out of the house and away with them sitting there. They would follow me. She had no choice. She casually closed and locked the front door, got in her car and sped off. They followed. The rain got worse and you could hardly see in front of the windscreen. She saw a police car driving behind them and slammed on her brakes. The men swerved and went up the kerb; the Police car stopped behind them and in her mirror, she saw the two officers get out and make their way to who would be followers. Gerty thought, that was lucky. She decided it was too risky going to her own home because they might already know the address and catch up with her again. She only had one place left and that was the business. She got back just as the rain stopped and a dark blanket covered the sky.

Bella caught a glimpse of Gerty just as she arrived and rushed to get her attention.

'Gerty (she threw her voice) I want yer advice.'

'Yes, ok how can I help?'

'I can't tink of a neme for dis pleace, any ideas?'

'Yes, The Lilly Club.'

Bella said in a high-pitched moan, 'Der Lilly Club. Wat kind of a neme is dat. It soundin like a prostitutes den.'

'How about the Shagging Palace?'

Bella could not believe what Gerty was saying, 'well, dats what dis plaes is.'

'I don't want it to sound that obvious. I've got it, The Poppy Club.'

'Ya meet as will carl it der opium Den.'

Gerty said as she was getting fed up, 'well what would the girls call it? Let's go ask 'em.'

They both walked into the lounge where most of them were watching telly.

Gerty said, 'we would like your attention. We need a name for this place but can't think of a good one. Any ideas?'

A little voice came from the corner of the room and Trudy said, 'The Passion flower Club.'

The room went quiet. Nobody said a thing.

Trudy went on to say, 'It doesn't sound like a prostitutes den, it sounds like a potting shed and for that it disguises the place. It's feminine and low key. We want all those things.'

Gerty raised her voice a little, applauded, and said, 'well done, it's perfect. If we are all agreed, The Passion Flower Club it is then.'

Bella walked off mumbling, 'Der Passion Flower Club, indeed.'

A lady was standing in reception trying to get some bodies attention. Wendy arrived and asked the woman how she could help. The woman asked to see the manager or owner. Wendy asked the lady to take a seat and she would enquire for her. Wendy found Bella and Gerty in the lounge still talking to the workers. Wendy politely beckoned them over with a hand gesture and told them about the lady in reception.

Gerty and Bella looked at each other; Gerty quizzically asked Bella, 'shall I get this one?'

'Be me guest.'

Gerty followed Wendy and she showed her to the woman.

Gerty said, 'would you like to talk in my office?'

The lady smiled and acknowledged, 'I don't mind if I do.'

Once in she asked the woman, 'how can we help?'

The lady came straight to the point and said, 'I am a Sex Therapist and would like to join your group. I have been told this place is a brothel and it would come in handy not only for my clientele but to study as well. Only if you are willing that is.'

Gerty sat down in her chair and said, 'what an unusual request.'

The woman carried on, 'I would like it to be a permanent arrangement and would like to hire some rooms out, if that is possible.'

Gerty thought for a moment.

Then said, 'I need to talk to the rest of my staff and get back to you. Would you be willing to come back in a couple of days?'

The woman said, 'my name is Georgie by the way and yes, I would be delighted.'

Gerty enthusiastically said, 'I will get my Manager to make the arrangements. Well, Georgie, nice to meet you and will be in touch.'

With that, Georgie thanked Gerty for her time and left the building. As Georgie walked out, Bella walked in.

She said, 'wat was dat all about den?'

'Maybe we're going professional. Therapeutism.'

Bella screwed her face up and with a blank fact to boot replied, 'whaaat?'

'She is a sex therapist that wants us to hire some of our rooms and also use our services for her studies.'

Bella excitedly commented, 'dat bi brilliant. When do she start?'

'I wanted to talk to everyone first and see what the girls think. Bella, call a meeting so we can discuss this openly with all of them.'

Bella replied with eagerness, 'right awey Ma'am.'

Bella came back as quick as she went and told Gerty, two this afternoon. Gerty had a few errands to run and a little book-keeping and banking to do.

Gerty got back in the nick of time. She hurried straight into the dining room where she heard voices and everyone was sitting around the huge dining table.

Bella said quietly to Wendy, 'keep yer eye in der reception, will ya?'

Wendy nodded and carried on looking at Gerty.

'Right girls, I'll get right to the point. I have been approached by a sex therapist.'

The girls went, 'woooooo, weeeee.'

Gerty carried on, 'she wants to rent out some of our rooms for her business. She would also like to have you girls help her with her research. That is up to you if you accept her here. This is a decision I am not willing to take without you. It's also that simple.'

Cara asked, 'will she pay us?'

Trudy said, 'what kind of research?'

Gerty replied, 'I don't know all the answers but perhaps you can call her in Bella, and ask her to answer all your questions. All I am interested in at present is, are we interested?'

The girls looked around at each other and then a thoughtful silence.

Cara replied, 'I think it's a good idea. People with sex problems need help and what better place than here.'

Trudy said simply, 'yes.' The two Asian girls replied, 'no problem.'

Wendy nodded and rushed to reception because the phone was ringing.

A DANGEROUS FLIGHT

Gerty finished with her meeting and asked Bella as they walked back to her office what she thought about how the meeting went?

Bella replied, 'it were good. Workers were up fer dat.'

Bella handed her some tickets and said, 'yer flight is tomorrow in de afta noon.'

Gerty stopped walking and looked at them.

'Tomorrow,' she replied.

Bella carried on walking, 'no time like de present.'

Gerty noticed that since she had been back, Bella had grabbed her confidence three fold. She was not the lady she used to know and felt quite proud of the fact of who she now was. Running this place was not easy but she had become a dab hand at it.

Three men walked into reception and saw Gerty standing there. Their eyes undressed her and all three wanted more. One tall, thickset man came over and gently put his arm around Gerty's waist. He spoke gently, 'are you new here? I haven't seen you around.'

Gerty replied softly, 'no but I have a lot to do.'

She smiled and removed his hand gently. With that, he stared as she walked off. Wendy asked who they were booked in with and could she see some I.D. Without taking his eyes off Gerty's body, he asked Wendy, 'who was that?'

Wendy whispered to him, 'that's the boss.'

His eyes lit up and his excitement became apparent. All the men were sent to their allotted workers.

Gerty spent the rest of the day packing her gorgeous new clothes and suitcases. She had problems closing them and had Bella used her weight to squash the lids together.

Gerty said, 'any problems, phone me.'

'No problem. Tanks for mekin me der manager. You had more fait in me dan I did.'

'To be quite honest Bella, I was desperate and needed you to be, but you have deserved it all. You have amazed me with your professionalism.'

She passed her an envelope and inside as she opened it was a cheque for three thousand pounds.

Bella's eyes nearly fell out and she said, 'I can't accept dis?'

Gerty went to snatch it back and said, 'alright I will . . . .'

Bella smiled with elation, 'alright, just dis once mind. Tanx.'

Bella gave Gerty a cuddle.

Gerty got a taxi to the airport and left her car at The Passion Flower Club. The girls waved good bye and said, till next time. The journey was about an hour and then a few more hours before takeoff. Gerty bought some lunch at the airport and settled with a gin and tonic in the lounge bar. She later browsed the duty free shops but didn't buy anything. She had already bought gifts from her shopping spree in Warwick.

Her time had come to board the plane and when she got to the airhostess, she said, 'sorry Ma'am but your seat has had to be used for another person but we have put you in first class. Is that all right?'

'That's fine.'

The hostess showed her to her new seat. Gerty was in her element. She had never travelled in first class before. She had always gone for economy to save money. Her seat was like a sofa and when the flight had taken off and everybody could take their belts off, she was offered champagne as a welcome to Air Mauritius. She was also given a menu to choose what she wanted for her lunch. She was also given a long list of duty free products she could buy that the economy didn't offer. This was a whole new ball game. There were also free magazines and newspapers all for the asking and without payment. The flight was going to take at least thirteen hours so Gerty made herself comfortable.

Three hours had past and she thought she would stretch her legs. Half way up the aisle a trolley that was being pushed by the hostesses was coming her way. She thought if she sort of squashed into an empty seat, she could possibly get past while they pushed the trolley through. It worked and Gerty carried on with her quest. She smiled at some passengers and ignored others. She struggled again to get past with the passengers that were returning to their allotted seats. Gerty had to squash into other unseated areas just to get past again. Gerty thought they would have considered this inconvenience when building the bloody plane. The next thought was built by men, made by skinny people and organized by insane management. The plane had food to be distributed, a shop to be publicised, drinks to be sold and lots and lots of money to be made. That is what it boiled down to, how many humans they could squash in one area, how much could they consume in one journey, how much they could healthily drink and lastly, how much duty free could they get the people to buy before they got off the plane. This business left no error for space, cleanliness, healthiness and mostly comforts ability. It just was simply an uncomfortable ride. Gerty hated flying but it was the quickest way to get to where she wanted to be.

She stopped at the aisle that her ticket number was and she noted the seat was empty. Then she noticed the seat next to hers had a woman that looked like Gerty but she looked to be fast asleep. Gerty checked the ticket again and the woman that was asleep was in fact in her seat. Gerty was asked by a passenger if she would move because he wanted to get past. Gerty obliged, turned around and started walking back to her seat. Gerty thought, why change her seat for someone exactly like me. It didn't add up. She expected somebody possibly disabled in some way, but there were no obvious signs. Anyway, she carried on to her seat and sat down.

A hostess came up to her and said, 'you're lunch Ma'am.'

Gerty looked up and replied, 'oh, errr, thank you.'

A table was laid in front of her with space all around. Metal knives and forks were put for her convenience. A glass for water and a glass for wine were laid side by side by her napkin and salt and pepper pots were placed in front of her. She was served with a roast chicken dinner and a lemon soufflé for desert.

She washed it down with a beautiful white crispy luscious pear flavoured light wine. The whole experience was mouth-wateringly splendid. The other people in first class were either talking to others or doing their own entertainment. Gerty was free from interaction and totally relaxed. She dozed for a couple of hours and when she woke up she noticed a familiar face but couldn't put a name to it. She was terrified and sat upright in her first class seat. She tried to hide herself from the onlooker. The shock was the realisation of the men in the car that chased her from her Mother's house. They were on the plane and a couple of seats away from her privacy. Panic struck her mind and turned it into anxiety stirred with the chicken running around in circles syndrome. This time she could only sit and think. Think and sit. She came up with a plan and asked the hostess for the duty free magazine. She also asked whether it was still alright to buy some products. The stewardess acknowledged a yes. Gerty looked through the things that could possibly disguise her. She saw a hat and some sunglasses. There were also silk scarves. She pointed out the ones she wanted to the hostess and within minutes Gerty was unwrapping them. She put them on and went for a walk to see if they could be fooled. It worked but she was not ready for what she saw further up the plane where she was supposed to have sat. She rushed to the toilet and shook on the toilet seat. As she past the woman that looked like her she noticed a knife sticking out the back of her chair and even though she looked as if she had dozed off. She was pale and dead.

Gerty thought, 'that knife was meant for me. Holy crap I have got to get off this plane.'

She studied her watch and counted how much longer she was going to be on the plane. She calculated thirty-two minutes. She could stay in here for about ten but she would have got to get back to her seat for touchdown and then be the first off the plane.

She waited until a knock came at the door. A passenger wanted to use the toilet.

Gerty thought, 'dam why now?'

She opened the door and slowly made her way back to her seat but she walked the other side this time so as not to walk past them again. Gerty sat down and asked the stewardess for a whisky and ginger ale with ice. She played with the drink in her mouth until all had gone. By that time, the captain was on the loud speaker asking passengers to put their seat belts on and the flight attendants were going along the aisles checking everyone was belted up properly and cleared away any containers such as glasses, rubbish, and any loose objects. Gerty gathered her belongings to the best of her ability so that she could make a quick get away when the plane landed. Gerty braced herself as the nose of the plane dived and tickled her tummy. Then, it levelled off a little and then the wheels screeched to an eventual halt. The plane carried on moving and Gerty realised they were being taken to one of those halls that connect to the plane so that the passengers could walk straight to the airport instead of being transported by bus or have to walk across the runway. Once connected and the doors opened, the staff acknowledged to the passengers that they had arrived and could vacate from the plane. They didn't have to tell Gerty twice, she was off like a rocket. Gerty rushed through the hallway, straight to the luggage escalators, picked up her luggage and through to customs and passport checks. She went through with no problem. She quickly checked behind just in case anybody was following her. She must have walked fast because she had left her plane buddies behind. She heard on the loud speaker for all passengers that had just come off the Birmingham flight to remain in the airport. Gerty thought sod that and rushed to find her taxi. The outside was very warm and had a distinct smell of flowers but with a distant odour of bad eggs. That could only be one thing and that was sulphur. A Mauritian Man was holding up her name and he came up as she acknowledged him and took her suitcases off her. She jumped in the car and they drove to The Lilly Palace Hotel.

Gerty did not tell her sons or parents that she was flying back so this trip was going to be a big surprise. The taxi driver pulled up in front of the Hotel and Joe with Grandma were talking to one of the receptionists. They glanced sideways and standing there was Gerty. Joe ran like mad and flung his arms round his Mom. Beth was delighted to see her daughter again and gave her a squeeze and a kiss on her cheek. They all walked to the reception desk and Gerty booked in. Beth had finished with the receptionist earlier and they all followed the porter to her original room. Gerty asked would they all come to her room as she had some presents to give everyone.

Gerty enquired, 'where's Dad?'

Beth and Joe said together, 'oh they've gone on a boat trip to fish.'

'Oh,' and carried on opening her suitcase.

She pulled out an expensive designer top for Joe. He revelled in it. He took off his top and exchanged it for his new one. He was so pleased.

'Mom that's for you,' as she pushed it towards her.

Gerty quickly took it back and took the price off the garment.

Beth stared with elation, 'this must have cost you a packet.'

'You're worth it.'

Gerty took two other items out the suitcase and laid them on the bed. Beth moved to the bathroom and came out with her new dress on. She loved it.

Joe took his old top and put it in his own room. While he was gone, Gerty found the opportunity to ask her Mom whether she had thought any more about where to live.

Beth said, 'your father and I always liked Greece. In fact, we liked Sidari, Corfu. Would it be possible to try something there?'

Gerty was happier knowing her parents were all right about living abroad for her sake as well as the boys and for themselves, hopefully.

The next few days were happy ones. With their reunited fun they splashed and enjoyed each other's company. They all left their worries behind them for a short time anyway.

SIDARI FOREVER

---⋆---

The next evening they all sat down as if it were their last super. All had agreed that it was time to find their new home and move on. Gerty spoke to a rep of Thomas Cook and they arranged everything; a flight, accommodation, food transport and taxis to and from the airports. Gerty paid by credit card.

They packed, they travelled, they arrived and they sank on their new found beds with jet lag. The whole environment was different. The air smelt heavy, hot and humid; almost a sandy, dusty mouthful. Everywhere was covered in greenery. The only place where you could see boulders, conifers and earth was the forests. The trees were so heavy with foliage that it was quite dark underneath and so not much growth of anything else. It took roughly two hours to get to the next hotel. The roads were all up hill and down dale with the occasional boulder to swerve around. The local drivers were ex Kamikaze pilots from the way they drove. They headed straight for their vehicle and swerved just in the nick of time, for a miss. Others drove too fast and slammed on their brakes for the hell of it and others just drove with missing brain cells. Luckily for them the taxi driver knew his people and was well aware of the dangers ahead.

They got there in one piece and to re-iterate sank into their beds with a backwards throw of the head, then body and then lifting of the feet. All were in no fit state to go anywhere, and fell asleep until next morning; which incidentally was a few hours away. The Hotel that they were staying at was called Heparins guild hotel. It was not as palatial as Mauritius but the circumstances were soon to change.

Gerty woke up and decided today was the day she started shopping for some premises. She walked down to her parents room and asked her mother if she would come shopping for a new home. Gerty also asked her Dad to watch the boys and as usual, he obliged.

Their first port of call was the estate agents. There were quite a few. There were also one or two property's that caught both their eyes. One was a half finished building in Sidari itself and a collection of apartments just on the outskirts of town. The prices were very reasonable. They both were able to look at them straight away. The first one that they were taken to had three acres of grounds surrounding the house. The house itself was not fully finished and needed doors, windows, electricity, and a roof.

The estate agent said, 'you need to think about the bigger picture and imagine it finished. I have the plans in the office. Would you like to look them?'

Gerty said, 'Uuummm, yes I am interested. What about skilled workers and are they reliable?'

The estate Agent enthusiastically replied, 'my family are in the trade and yes they are very reliable. They also know the legalities of building in Greece which could come in handy.'

Gerty was impressed and said in her business tones, 'will they bring their price down any lower, because of the work I would have to pay for would be plenty?'

The estate agent replied, 'yes, indeed. He wants shot of it and as quickly as possible.'

Beth asked, 'how long would it take before it is habitable, from buying to finishing to living in?'

The estate agent said, 'with the right builder's maybe you are looking at six to eight months.'

Gerty gave her a very low price from the asking price and asked her to talk it over with the owner.

Next was a collection of apartments. There were four in all and each one was a holiday home. The owner of these was in financial ruin. He would take anything for them just to get them off his hands. They had also been on the market for roughly two years. So his name was fast becoming desperate Dan. Again, after looking at each apartment Beth said, 'yes please Gerty. We can live in these until the other building is completed.'

This place was also in a secluded spot with roughly two acres around the property and room to build a swimming pool. Beth this time looked at Gerty and gave a ridiculously low offer for the estate Agent to negotiate. Beth asked, 'how long will it take to buy this one. It depends on whether he wants to sell and the land registry plus the solicitors involved.

Beth said, 'can you ask the owner if we could rent the apartments while we are in negotiations with him?'

Gerty looked surprised at her Mother and smiled.

They were taken back to the hotel by the estate agent and told she would contact them in a few days. Gerty and Beth were so excited and told the others what they had been up to.

John asked, 'will we ever go back to England?'

Gerty looked sorrowfully at John and replied, 'one day when the coast is clear. The first thing I need to do is get you into your new schools here.'

Gerty knew nothing and asked reception. They were very helpful and Gerty went to have a chat with the local school Head master. It was by appointment and Gerty had a short sharp shock when she entered the gates. The school was very run down indeed. The play ground was antiquated and there was no school uniform. She didn't stop for the appointment; in fact she never walked through the gates. It repulsed her so much she just couldn't do that to her boys. Gerty decided that while she was in town she would have a look around. She was hungry but didn't want to go back just yet. Her mission had not been completed and she found herself on a mission impossible. She sat in a cafe and asked for their speciality which was a Donna kebab and their local tea. She off the cuff asked if there were any decent schools in the area and was pointed into the direction of the town. Gerty followed the instructions and low and behold a decent looking school standing in front of her. Gerty went to what looked like the entrance of the school and asked about her boys being in the school. The Head Master invited her into his office and after a lengthy discussion was told they could start Monday next. Gerty could have kissed him, but didn't.

She got to the boys and told them the good news. They were not impressed at all. They thought that this was going to be a permanent holiday and that school was a thing of the past. Both went to their rooms showing their distaste for the inevitable.

Trevor quietly gestured to Gerty, 'I'll talk to them.'

Gerty used her resources and bought both the premises at a fantastic price. They were able to move and rent the intended apartments that they now were buying. Work got underway at the new house and her life was finally pulling together in the right direction.

DEATH THREAT

—✦—

One Saturday afternoon she was tired, exhausted with the tension of everything happening around her. The apartments were finished and they could move into the last one. The house was looking like a high class mansion. It looked so much better than the plans. There were still a few tidy ups to be managed before the final move to their new home. She decided to take time out and went shopping in the town. First, she went for a coffee in a local cafe. She noticed some Men and thought they were following her but when she got up, paid the bill and went shopping they were nowhere to be seen. She was just about to catch the local bus to get back when she was grabbed from behind and bundled fiercely into a Volkswagen dormobile. The whole van was painted black, even the windows. Her hands were tied behind her and a bag was put on her head and she could hardly breathe. She had a panic attack and her breathing felt as if it were going to stop. She was hit in the stomach and told to sit still. She could feel other people sitting beside her but they seemed smaller somehow. She was petrified and did not move a muscle until it seemed half an hour later. There was a distinct stale body odour of men that had perspired but that hadn't washed for days. She wanted to vomit, as they were so close.

She thought she heard a child snivelling and heard a man spit shut up snivelling. He then hit the child because she was pushed into the side of Gerty's ribs. When Gerty was taken, all her belongings, handbag, shopping and her personal stuff was dropped to the ground. They must have travelled for hours because when they got there it was dark. They were in the middle of nowhere. The captives were taken still with their headgear on into a house and pushed down to a small room. Gerty sat on the floor not moving until eventually she could hear nothing. She gently moved her legs and sat up against the wall. The child was crying softly with terrifying trembles in her voice. Gerty slowly put her hands on the bag on her head and removed it. Gerty had been crying too and her makeup had smudged. She saw four other girls with her. One was about nine. She was the one crying and the others were about twelve and fifteen.

Gerty said quietly to each girl, 'I am going to remove the bags. It's alright.'

Gerty took the first one off with a trembling hand and it got easier as she lifted the others. The room was dusty but clean. The window was so dirty that they couldn't see anything through it. All of them stayed in that room over night. Gerty suddenly realised that she could hear somebody coming. She quickly told everyone to put their bags back on their heads, which they did. Two tanned pot bellied men entered the room. They were small in stature and nearly bald.

The first man said, 'you do as you are told and you won't get hurt.'

The second man growled and spat, 'if you don't behave yourself you will get this and a beating with my special whip.'

He was holding his crotch when he said this and the other man laughed. Nobody said a thing.

Nobody moved a muscle but the little girl wet herself and the first man got hold of her arm and said, 'you dirty slut. You're coming with me.'

He dragged her by her hair down the corridor. She screamed, was hit, and told to shut up. Gerty was disgusted but said nothing afraid if she did she would be next. It did not make any difference. The second man grabbed Gerty by the hair and took her to another room. Another man was waiting. He bent her over a barred bed and gave her full penetration. She suffered in silence knowing that if she said anything she would be in more trouble.

Gerty found herself and the other girls getting used to being humiliated, beaten and totally demoralised by a collection of men. She could see no obvious way out. After all this, she was relieved because she thought she was being grabbed because of the death threats but finally realised that she was grabbed at random in the street to be worked by a gang of Paedophiles and gang prostituers. Gerty also realised some of the girls were far too young and nobody should do anything like this against their will, it was barbaric.

Gerty was taken to another place and this time she was not bagged. The outside of the building was like a rural farm land. She saw a church in the distance and thought of her loving brother. She also thought when she gets back to normality she would ask for his help to also help these girls.

After travelling for hours Gerty saw an old run down church in the middle of fields. Women were harvesting the fields and the men put their produce on carts that were pulled by donkeys. The man that she was travelling with told her to step down. He pushed Gerty to the door and a Nun answered it. Gerty was taken to a room with a bed in it. She heard a phone go off and the sound was of The Beatles song Maggie Mae. She almost fell with shock when she looked around and saw her brother taking two young girls down the corridor. Gerty wanted to cry out but she knew that if she did her brother would be in an uncompromising position. She decided to try and get his attention later when nobody could see or hear, maybe? The nun closed and locked the door. Gerty's sore eyes flowed with tears. It had been nearly a month since she was first attacked and pushed into the van. Surely someone would be looking for her by now. She sat on the bed and reality kicked in. She was never gonna get through this. She was never gonna get out of there. Her life was in tatters. The only thing she was sure of is her family was safe. Safe for now anyway. She wasn't really bothered about the sexual abuse because of being a prostitute she could handle it. She did not like the abuse but tolerated it. What she found hard to cope with was the lack of control she had. She did not have a choice and different men wanted different things. She obliged for her life. One of the problems she couldn't cope with was realising the young girls of such a tender age whipped, brutally treated and groomed for their potential market and profit. It was definitely a cold, callous business run by cut throat thugs, murderers and inhumane bullies. Some of the young girls were treated like dogs. After seeing the treatment that all the women had to put up with Gerty wanted revenge, not just for her but for all women forced to have sex with no tenderness, passion, caring or respect. Gerty laid down on the thin mattress and fell asleep.

She was awake waiting for her next thug to abuse her. The door opened at dawn and a Nun told her without conversation to follow her. Gerty thought that she could have done with a warm shower with soap instead of a wash down with a dirty rag and a cold bucket of water. Her arm had red itchy dots on the shoulder and that could only mean one thing, bed bugs, huge ones. She scratched but the itching became worse. Her shoulder was inflamed with the mites. She stopped scratching and was taken into a long room with a massive table that had many chairs. She was told to sit and the Nun brought her a bowl of what looked like porridge. It tasted of oats without the sugar and quite coarse but it was just barely palatable. Gerty was so hungry she ate like there was no tomorrow. She was given some pieces of bread that had been broken by hand, with a glass of milk. This place was very unkempt. The windows were faded with years of weathered grime. The floor had insects crawling. The only insect free place was the table surface. The building needed much work doing to it. There were bullet holes in the walls behind her. The smell, dusty with bodily sweat. Gerty felt so intensely dirty, grubby and just wanted to wash away this place. Up the other end of the room, she saw some thick, stocky men moving toward her.

She thought, 'oh god, this is the next phase of dread. With her clothes stained, dirty and worn where she had knelt or fallen thought, how could these men possibly want sex with her in such a filthy state?'

One of the thugs shouted, 'on your feet tramp.'

The other grabbed her breast and said to the other, 'not much meat,' then he let her go.

The both men followed her and laughed at what they had just said. Gerty kept herself to herself and did not acknowledge any emotion. There was a room just around the corner from the dining room. It had a single bed with a metal frame and a very thin mattress. It also had one very dirty ground in dirt pillow. There was a table nearly waist height and two chairs. When they arrived Gerty was told to sit on one of the chairs. The thugs waited. After about five minutes, a young girl of about eighteen walked trembling into the room and told to sit on the other chair.

The two thugs started, smiling and said to the young girl, 'this is your first sex lesson.'

The both men started laughing. They both suddenly stopped and grabbed Gerty by her hair and threw her into the corner of the room.

The other Man demanded, 'strip off everything.'

He said it slowly and precisely. The both men stood over her and watched as each garment was peeled off her body.

One of the thugs tossed a coin into the air and one said, 'it's your lucky day.'

Gerty did not know which one was going to have her pleasure until the stocky, pot bellied one said, 'take your body over to the table and bend over with your legs stretched well apart.'

Gerty was trembling not knowing what he had planned. The girl sitting was grabbed by her hair and put into a position where she could see all the activities slowly.

The thug could see that Gerty was ready and he said as he opened the zip of his trousers and flopped his semi flaccid cock out, 'this master piece is going to be pushed into this hole here.'

His finger went into her vagina and he wiggled it about. The thug said as his bulging mass was at full strength, 'It goes in like this.'

The girl tried to look away. She was embarrassed and felt disgusted but she could not move because the Man held her down. Gerty gave no sign of emotion as the thug carried on his quest.

The thug said, 'now it's in, we as masters keep sliding in and out until we blast you with our powerful spunk.'

He used up all his energy until he was exhausted and released his fluid. Gerty looked board and was glad it was all over.

Gerty stood up slowly and asked, 'could she wash.' The thug shouted, 'no you slut, put your clothes on.'

The Man holding the young girl by her hair said, 'now it's your turn.'

He let go of her hair and shouted yet again, 'take your fucking clothes off.'

The girl looked at Gerty and started crying and still trembling.

Gerty whispered, 'just imagine you are on a beach holiday somewhere. It won't take long.'

Gerty was told to sit down and watch by the same thug who had just performed on her.

The girl bent over and spread her legs. The other Man that was holding her hair previously was the master this time. He prepared her and pushed himself inside her but the girl found it too painful and moved forward. His knob fell out and he knee'd her in the back. He told her to stand up but she did not do it fast enough. He kicked her in the stomach. She screamed with pain. He got down and punched her in the face. Gerty was stressed to see a young girl treated so. She went to move but the other thug grabbed her hair so she could not. The other thug was still attacking the young girl. He stopped after many punches. He told her to get up and demanded they start again. She did not move.

He shouted, 'get up.'

He kicked her again. She didn't move. He turned her over and she was limp.

Gerty looked at her and said, 'I think she's dead. You killed her.'

He growled, 'shut up, bitch.'

The other Man let go of Gerty's hair and went over to the girl lying lifeless on the floor.

He looked at the other thug and said quietly, 'I think she's dead.'

The thugs thought for a minute, one went out, and within a minute, her brother was brought into the room. Her brother said to the thugs, 'burn the body, then crush the bones with that new machine. Lloyd looked at Gerty but she was so dirty he didn't recognise her and Gerty looked away.

Lloyd carried on by saying, 'have you found my sister yet. Have you tracked down where they've moved to?'

Gerty really wanted to damage him. She suddenly knew the threats; her son's finger was a set up by her brother. She was roaring with rage, anger, hurt and betrayal. She sat there looking at the floor, terrified to look up. Lloyd left the room. The thugs ordered a Nun to take Gerty back to her room.

Gerty cried like she never did before. Tears for her brother the way they used to be. She could not believe the betrayal, the hurt, the shear deception of his life. A godly man with the path to Christ. How could he treat human beings this way and why? What made him this way? She slept very little that night. The next morning it was the same routine. The same men and the same room. Another girl was pushed into the room and Gerty was told to take her dirty clothes off. She still had the fluid in her jeans from yesterday and the sweat of the thug from yesterday on her skin.

The other thug held the other girls hair as before. Gerty saw a metal pole lent against the wall where she was to take her clothes off. She grabbed it and with full force bounced the pole off the thugs head. He hit the deck unconsciously. The other thug was still holding the hair of the girl. The girl elbowed him and he was winded which made him let go. Gerty flung full throttle with all her force again and knocked him to the ground. He got up in a daze and tried to grab Gerty's arms. Gerty gave an almighty blow and the man fell to the ground. The both thugs had guns in their pockets but Gerty was so fast they did not have time to use them. She gave one gun to the other girl and said, 'I have never used one of these but we need to be quick learners if we are to survive.'

Gerty took the lead and crept out to the corridor. She could see her brother across the court yard. She told the girl to run away from her through the court yard and through the big doors to the great outdoors. She also explained she had unfinished business.

The girl said, 'we won't get out of here unless we stick together.'

Gerty replied, 'ummmm quite possibly. Come on then.'

They both ran through the courtyard and hid in one of the empty rooms. Gerty heard her brother coming closer. He was talking to a couple of his accomplices. She could see him and called his name quietly. She saw Lloyd come into the room followed by his two stooges. Gerty held the gun up close to her face ready to fire. Lloyd looked into the room and straight into the barrel of the gun. The two stooges followed. The girl shot both stooges in the legs and they fell to their knees. Lloyd was bewildered and surprised.

Gerty said, 'hi bro haven't seen you in a long time. How are you?'

Lloyd said, 'what are you doing here? How did you find me? What the fuck is she doing shooting my parishioners?'

Gerty raged, 'what the fuck are you doing cutting the finger of my son off and leaving sick threats for me?'

As she raged, she also shot her brother in the leg. Lloyd went to grab her, the girl shot Lloyd in the chest, and one bullet went into his groin.

Lloyd replied, 'what are you talking about? I wouldn't do that.'

Gerty fiercely roared, 'no, I can see you have your gang to do the dirty work for you. I've been well and truly fucked by you and now it's your turn.'

Gerty pulled the trigger and put a bullet in his head. He fell instantly to the ground with his eyes rolling backwards. It was like a slow motion decent and then a big boom as his body hit the dusty deck. The girl shot the two stooges in the head and Gerty heard people running.

Gerty said, 'quick, we got to get out of here.'

There was no way out. The room had only one exit and that was in front of them. Gerty could hear people trying to find out where the shooting noise was coming from.

Gerty said, 'Quick put one body in the wardrobe and one body under the bed, I have a plan.'

The girl said, 'what about this one?'

Gerty said, 'I have a plan for that one. Hide behind that wardrobe.'

The girl did as she was told. Gerty put one of the stooges on top of her in the bed and stripped to the waist. When anybody came in they would see a couple having sex in the bed. Gerty lay there with her breasts out of the blanket showing all. The body was put in such a position it looked as if the person under the bed was giving her oral. A Nun came in, looked, and then went. A couple of men came in looked, then went. They must have been so used to this kind of behaviour that they never saw the blood on the floor. Twenty minutes went by and the talking stopped. Gerty told the girl that they needed to dispose of the body.

The girl said, 'I know where we can get some Nun's habits from.'

She crept out of the room and was back in minutes.

She said, 'here, put this on.'

Gerty said, 'we look the part in this. My idea is to get rid of the bodies as they would. First we need to find where they burn the bodies.'

The girl said, 'I know, follow me.'

Gerty said, 'you are forgetting one thing?'

The girl replied, 'what?'

Gerty said sarcastically, 'the bodies?'

The girl said, 'no, I haven't. If we are to do this we need the equipment to do this and to make it look good. Just follow me.'

Gerty said nothing and just followed. They came back with a man made wheel barrow just for this occasion. It was made of long struts of wood, held together by rounded pieces of metal around the outside and bottled together with huge ferry bolts. It had a very long dragging handle and bicycle wheels. It was well made and made to last. It looked to be originally made for the harvest workers outside the church grounds.

The bodies were very heavy but between them they managed to get them on the barrow. The girl knew where to go and the furnace was blazing away.

The girl said sheepishly, 'you need to cut the bodies up and put them into the furnace.'

Gerty said, 'you mean, we?'

The girl felt she had no choice and they cut them up into manageable chunks. The burning went on for hours and both girls were extremely tired. The girl said she would keep watch while Gerty got some sleep. Gerty went out like a light. When she woke she thought where was she. The girl was getting the bones out of the cinders and putting them into a bucket. All three men's bones fitted into a conventional sized bucket. Gerty thought of her brother and then thought she hadn't got time for sentiment and so wiped her tears. The girl carried the bucket to the grinding machine that was located outside in the yard. She put it on and ground down all that was left of the men. Gerty could hear somebody coming their way and then saw them hurrying towards them. It was a farm worker. She came over with rage and turned off the machine. Gerty and the girl had finished anyway. They laughed with surprise because they thought they would get caught with the Nun's habits on. The evening light was going and freedom was literally around the corner. The girl and Gerty walked for miles. They both didn't know where they were but they didn't care. It was freedom.

On their journey, they hid from quite a number of cars going to the church they had just escaped from. The walk to the nearest town went to Nymfes. This was quite a built up area but nobody spoke English and there was no phone. Gerty and the Girl hitched a ride on the back of a cart heading towards Sidari. Gerty asked the driver and he pointed the way to Sidari. They got on his cart and started the long journey. At a place called Episopi, which was a small village the man politely told them that he would arrange for them to travel by another transport that would take them to Aglii Douli. This next journey was longer than this had taken and they would not get there until midnight. The transport though was a lorry and they were able to sleep in the back. Because of their habit's they were treated with the greatest respect. It was pitch black when they arrived and the lorry driver pulled over and went and asked another lorry driver to take them to Sidari. He obliged and Gerty with the girl sat in the front of the lorry by the side of the driver. He could smell their body odour and tried to stay away from them. There was not much conversation but he drove faster than the other men and that meant getting to Sidari quicker.

The next village was Esperies and then they saw the signs for Sidari. The lorry was delivering some boxes to a warehouse on the outskirts of Sidari and dropped them off not far, from where Gerty had bought her apartments. They walked the distance home. Gerty did not know what time it was but she did not even care. She had been kidnapped without ransom for over two months and was glad to be alive and back with her family. She knocked on the door to her Mom's apartment. No answer. She knocked again. No answer. The occupiers of the apartment next door came out and tried to make a scene. Gerty asked where the man and woman with two boys had gone. They told her that they lived on the other side of town in one of the big houses that had just been finished building. Gerty apologised for their inconvenience and the lady curtsied to the Nun's. Gerty and the girl walked away.

Half way down the street Gerty said, 'we have got about a mile to walk, and then home sweet home.'

The girl said, 'my home is in Bulgaria. How am I going to get back there?'

Gerty said, 'well I might have a plan, but we need to get you a passport first.'

Finally, they reached the front door of her newly finished home. She knocked and her mother opened it.

On their arrival Beth said, 'why are you here at this ungodly hour?'

Gerty started to cry and said, 'Mom it's me, Gerty.'

Beth screamed with delight and all the lights went on in the house. The boys were standing on the top of the landing and raced down the stairs as soon as they knew it was their gorgeous Mom. Trevor started to cry and put his arms around Gerty.

He cried, 'where have you been? What have you been doing? Why are you dressed like a Nun?'

He then pulled away and said, 'girl you wreak. Have you been working with pigs? Come in, come in.'

Gerty suddenly remembered the girl and started to introduce her to her parents, 'Mom and Dad this is uuummmmmmm, I don't even know your name?'

The girl said with a smile, 'my name is Rosa.'

Gerty carried on saying, 'Rosa, this is my Mom and Dad. These are my boys, Joe and John.'

THE CHANGE

Suddenly it was party night. Beth got food out. Trevor showed them where the bathroom was and Beth told Gerty that she had put her in the front bedroom. Rosa and Gerty both had a lovely long soak in the bath. One bathroom was joined to Gerty's room and the other was the family bathroom where Rosa melted into clean water with the aroma of beautiful bubble bath and clean towels. Gerty gave her some clothes to put on. They were similar in build but Gerty was slightly taller. The night was paradise in a new home.

For the next few weeks Gerty didn't venture very far. She had been traumatised more than she knew. Rosa too but for her she was young and quite level headed. Rosa plodded along with what Gerty was doing and her life was put on hold.

Gerty lived on the money from her business in England. It was booming. Profits were high and things were running well for a change. Now that there were no more threats to her family, Gerty was ready to ask her family to choose where they really wanted to be. She arranged for her Mom and Dad to go back and stay in England for a couple of weeks. She wanted them to check their property and to see friends that they hadn't seen for over a year. Joe and John wanted to go too.

Gerty said, 'another time maybe. We could all go back together next year.'

John said, 'Mom, I miss my friends.'

'Why don't you ask your friends to come over here for a holiday? They could stay for a couple of weeks. I'll pay.'

John said in disbelief, 'really?'

'Write to them or better still phone.'

Gerty was not the same woman from two years ago. Her mental state had been turned upside down. Her way of thinking had been fully tested to its limits, even the way she thought of prostitution had somehow been battered and re-adjusted into, she did not know what. Her way of life was in tatters.

She decided she had bought the apartments to rent out but to use one or two of them for prostitution. She had apartments available and went out into the streets of Sidari and discussed her ideas with the help of a couple of prostitutes on known street corners who spoke broken English. Gerty also found out she was in new territory. There were pimps controlling every corner. She went home wondering whether her line of business was going to work here at all. She thought for now she would play it safe and rent the apartments as holiday flats. It would also give her time to make money and think about the future and her family. Gerty gave Rosa a job keeping the apartments up to a good clean standard. Rosa lived in one of the apartments and worked as a chambermaid, plus be Gerty's representative to the guests that stayed. This worked a dream and within no time, Rosa was working and content with her line of business. Gerty was happy she was legitimately running a business with a good reputation for a change with no hassle.

Gerty spent the next three years just playing Mom. Her daily chores were doing the washing, ironing, and general housekeeping. She pottered around the garden and tidied the boarders. Her parents would take a walk down to the beach and sometimes go swimming with the boys when they were not at school. The boys made a lot of friends and sometimes ate at the local restaurants that were scattered in the bays for lunch. Gerty would phone Bella occasionally and just gossip about the business or themselves.

GERTY NEVER THOUGHT THAT WOULD HAPPEN

———◆———

Gerty decided to check on the apartments and visited Rosa. She found Rosa to be a sweet young lady that was always willing to help and muck in when needed. Gerty told her never to tell a soul about anything about who they shot, what they did or even where the place was. Once the secret was locked, it was never to be opened again by anyone and the pact was made.

Gerty decided it was time that Rosa found out about her family and asked, 'Rosa, have you ever wondered about going home to your family?'

Rosa replied with sad eyes, 'oh yes, all the time. It's been a long time since I saw them.'

Gerty said, 'if you give me the address I will make arrangements for you to go home for three weeks at the end of this month.'

Rosa started to cry and blubbered, 'oh thank you.' Rosa wrote the address down there and then. She handed it to Gerty and they spoke about having a swimming pool for the guests in the apartments back garden.

The end of the month came. Gerty had brought Rosa's tickets and gave her some extra spending money on top of her wages as a thank you for her help. Gerty liked Rosa a lot and felt she was almost like her big sister. Gerty had never had a sister only a nasty brother, which she thought the world of. On the day of the flight Gerty ordered a taxi to take Rosa to the airport, gave her the spending money, passport, and kissed her good bye. She also asked her to come back. Gerty felt she had done a good turn for Rosa, which made Gerty feel good inside.

Life still carried on feeling better and three weeks on Gerty was looking forward to having Rosa back. The day before Rosa's return Gerty walked into town and sat alone in her favourite restaurant. Sometimes she liked her own company but tonight it wasn't to be. She heard a familiar voice and looked round. A couple of tables away were four men sitting, chatting, and eating. They all looked very tanned and almost overdone. One man instantly recognised Gerty and stood up. Gerty suddenly realised it was Michael. With that she called the waiter over and cancelled the rest of her meal. The waiter was not very happy but she just wanted to get out of there. Seeing Michael cut like a knife in her heart. She simply loved him so much many years ago and he just left. She had never seen him again until now.

Michael on the other hand cared for her deeply when they were together but he was destroyed almost by finding out that she was a prostitute. He could not believe his future wife was sleeping with possibly dozens of men a day while he was at work. That was then but this is know. His morals were still the same but his heart started pounding when he saw her. He quickly dropped everything and rushed over to stop her leaving.

'Gerty,' he cried, 'Wait.'

Gerty carried on walking.

He ran and gently grabbed her arm, 'Gerty, please wait.'

Gerty looked down at the floor and cried, 'leave me alone.'

Michael didn't let go but replied, 'are you on holiday? Come and join us.'

Gerty said, 'you wouldn't want to be seen with a pro now, would you?'

Gerty slowly looked at him as she spoke.

Michael said, 'walk with me then. Tell me what you are doing here?'

Gerty said, 'I live here. Now can I go?'

She ran off. All she wanted to do was crawl under a rock and disappear. That was not like Gerty. She was such a strong, self willed person. Michael made her weak and vulnerable. She had to get away from that because she found it hard to handle.

Her emotions had been crushed, churned around and spat out into no particular order. It was horrible and she could not take it. She ran crying all the way home and locked herself in her room before anybody saw her. Beth went upstairs to enquire if Gerty was alright. Gerty changed her emotion to not show her mother that she was upset. It worked because her Mom went downstairs and told Trevor everything was alright. But inside Beth was not convinced. Gerty sprawled across the bed, belly down and cried herself to sleep. When she awoke it was seven thirty in the morning. She stayed home and pottered around the garden, then she tidied the house and finally went to the shops where she was hoping to bump into him again. She knew she hadn't forgotten him and wanted to see him for one last time. Gerty decided to eat at the same place for an afternoon snack. She sat in a corner of the restaurant outside and ordered a small cake with a cup of coffee. She looked around but no joy. She noticed the men with Michael walking past and thought he would be with them, but no Michael. She ate and waited. She drank and waited. She waited and waited. She decided it was no use and got up only to be tapped on the shoulder. Michael was standing behind her and asking to sit with her. She quietly nodded and he sat down.

He said, 'that night I heard that horrible thug talking to you and telling me you were a pro, I was devastated. I had left my wife and girl's for you. I had given up everything to be with you and you never told me anything.'

Gerty sat back and replied, 'what was I supposed to say, Hi Michael, I am a prostitute and shag men for a living? Or Hi Michael join the fucking queue?'

Michael called the waiter over and ordered more coffee.

Gerty asked, 'what are you doing here anyway?'

'I am on a bachelor holiday with my mates. We are all-single and thought we could have a fun holiday over here; and no, it's not like that Gerty. We're here for sand, sea, and socialising.'

Gerty said, 'no sex then?'

Michael replied as he looked at Gerty with one eye, 'maybe?'

Gerty said, 'I seem to remember you were good at that.'

Michael blushed and replied, 'where do you live then?'

Gerty said, 'not far. In fact, just around the corner from here. The boys were angry because you just ran out on them. It might not be a good idea you coming back to the house. I also live with my Mom and Dad.'

Michael replied, 'I missed you and would like to see more of you.'

Gerty said, 'is that between clients?'

Michael thought and replied, 'it's something we could work on.'

'Since seeing you last night I can't sleep, can't eat and can't do anything. I want you back.'

Gerty said, 'yeah, for a good shag. Anyway I've given all that up. I run a healthy apartment business now. All the other business is set up in England and I just collect the profits.'

Michael's friends came to collect him.

Michael said, 'I have got to go on an excursion and can't get out of it. Can I see you tonight?'

Gerty thought but said nothing.

Michael said, 'Gerty, meet me here tonight at about eight. For old time sake then. Say yes?'

Gerty replied with a sneaky smile, 'maybe, maybe not.'

Michael shouted as he was pulled away by his friends, 'eight?'

Gerty wanted to get up and go with them but she knew it would not be a good idea. All those men and little old her, Nahhhhhh.

Gerty turned up that night but Michael did not. Instead one of his mates told her that Michael had fallen on the excursion and broken his ankle. He was in hospital recovering from an operation. Gerty went with his mate straight to the hospital. It was not long before she felt so sorry for him and melted into his arms.

Gerty said, 'I never expected a date like this. You'll do anything for my attention, won't you?'

Michael pulled her close and replied, 'anything,' then kissed her.

Gerty felt tears roll down her face and she welled with emotion. She loved him so much and always did. Michael's bachelor boys left them alone until it was time for everyone to go home. Next day Gerty was up at the crack of dawn. She was in love, with all the additives, mindless thoughtlessness; not thinking straight and not thinking enough. Basically her mental state was in a cloud. Gerty told her family that she had bumped into Michael while he was on a bachelor holiday with friends and that he would be convalescing there for the next couple of weeks. Nobody was happy. Everybody grumbled about the way he just walked out all those years ago and had said nothing to anybody.

Gerty knew that her next visit to the hospital would possibly be to bring Michael to convalesce at her house. She also wanted him to live with her permanently. How could she ask, how would he react to that and why shouldn't he? She bought him an English paper to read and put it down by his side and then kissed him wantingly.

'The Doctor told me in his broken English said that I can go home today.'

Gerty hesitantly said, 'home to mine?'

'What to play doctors and nurses?'

Gerty hesitantly and shyly blushed, 'No, silly. Move permanently in with us.'

Michael glowed with wanting and quietly replied, 'really? Can I? Please can we be together forever?'

Gerty welled with tears and blubbered, 'yes please.'

Michael started to get out of bed. 'Right we're off. Take me woman to your kingdom.'

Gerty chuckled, her emotions were of love for Michael, and nothing else mattered. The nurse walked in and told Michael he needed to get back into bed. His blood results had come back abnormal and his leg was infected. She told him the Doctor would not let him go until all was clear. Gerty looked at Michael and said, 'a few more days would not hurt our togetherness.'

Michael chuckled, 'absence makes the heart get stronger and all that crap?'

Michael's friends handed over Michael's luggage to Gerty at her home because Michael told them he would be stopping in Corfu after the holiday and moving in with Gerty. The friends knew that Gerty was an old flame, just did not know how hot. Nothing had ever been mentioned about her prostitution and why they split up.

Rosa arrived back and knocked on Gerty's door. Beth answered and was so pleased to see her. Beth asked how she got on at home.

Rosa replied, 'very sad, my father died just after I disappeared from a heart attack. They say it was caused by my abduction. My mother is struggling without him and I said I would help by sending her some money. She told me my brother lost his legs in a motorbike accident and can't work. I am now their only hope for survival. I asked them to come and live with me but they say their family and home is Bulgaria.'

Beth said, 'you will be able to go back again another day. Are you glad you went, Rosa?'

Rosa started crying, 'yes and no. My father died and I loved him so, but my family is still alive and now they know I am safe it will stop them worrying so they can finally get on with their lives. I also want to make it easier for them, you know?'

Beth replied with an endearing smile, 'yes Rosa, I know.'

Gerty walked in just as the conversation stopped and gave Rosa a huge hug in amazement of seeing her again. Gerty was so excited and Rosa had to tell her story all over again. Finally Gerty took Rosa home to the apartment and told her it was good to have her back.

After Michael's convalescence in hospital, he was sent home. Gerty went and picked him up in her new car, a red Fiesta. They discussed how the family would provoke his presence and Gerty gently replied, 'they are my family and not my keepers. What we do with our lives is our business, what happened between us is our business and stays our business. My Mom and Dad know the truth and Mom is none too clever about it but she will come around eventually. Dad is quite easy going and will not take much time to accept the way we are. The boys are a different kettle of fish. They were badly hurt and thought for some reason, I don't know what, that it was their fault. We will be together forever this time?'

Michael re-iterated, 'forever and ever.'

Gerty said, 'that's what matters, our happiness thrown in with theirs, eventually to make one big happy family.'

Michael said, 'I had better hold my breath for a couple of months then.'

Gerty replied, 'maybe, we are doing this together, right?'

Michael smiled and gave her an engaging kiss on her cheek and then they were off.

It did take about six months for Michael and the boys to get to know each other once again. Their confidence grew and Michael being such a nice guy won them over, Gerty had never doubted the outcome.

Michael was also a big asset to the business. He had money of his own and bought a small hotel on the far side of Sidari. This Hotel was on the sea shore practically. He needed to make many changes. Gerty helped with decor and staffing ideas. It was slow to get going but after a few years picked up to a profit making, well organized business. Gerty and Michael were proud of their lives and very much in love. The boys grew up to be boisterous young men with girlfriends, friends, and a social life all over Sidari. The boys also had a reputation for being business minded, spoke the Greek language fluently, and smart. For the local ladies a gorgeous catch for the local families. In fact the locals were infatuated with their presence. John was now twenty two and Joe was eighteen years old.

COULD IT BE
WEDDING BELLS?

John worked in a restaurant, only a few miles from where they lived. He suggested that Gerty and Michael had a special, just the two of them, cosy, romantic night together with no interruptions at his work place. So, Gerty invited Michael out on a date, which they had not had for many years. She told him to dress smart because it was going to be a special occasion.

He wondered what it would be, 'maybe she wants to marry me, maybe a new business venture, maybe she's pregnant or I don't know what.'

He dressed to thrill. He wore a dark brown suit, a multi-coloured tie with tiny squares that was not too flash but sexy. He had a short sleeved pale green shirt with dark brown plastic rose shaped buttons on. His dark brown brogues were laced and shone like mirrors, they were glaringly polished. When he came out of the bedroom Beth stood aback and just stood with her mouth open as he walked down the corridor.

Michael looked back and said, 'Beth, do I look that good then?'

Michael laughed and Beth smiled and replied, 'Michael, if I were many years younger?'

Trevor came from the living room and said, 'Michael you've got to go.'

Michael was startled and replied, 'why?'

Trevor answered with a grin, 'we can't have two good looking men in this building. It's too much for our women folk.'

They both howled with laughter.

Michael was just about to go through the door when Trevor said, 'have a lovely evening, won't you?'

Michael said, 'D'you know what it's all about then?'

Trevor said, 'no, but it must be important to Gerty because she is dressed just as gorgeous as you are nearly.'

With that thought, Michael stepped into the taxi that Gerty had booked earlier.

Gerty got to the restaurant early and asked John what this was all about.

John replied, all in good time.'

John showed Gerty to her seat and she waited on her own. Gerty could see that John was talking to a young lady in the restaurant.

Gerty thought, 'she looks nice. I wonder whether that was his girlfriend.'

Michael arrived and John met him too and sat him by Gerty. Michael reached over to Gerty kissed her on her cheek and whispered, 'you look amazing.'

Gerty replied with a glowing Smile of admiration, 'you look better than me. How come you look so disgustingly edible?'

Michael replied with his charisma, 'oh, it was nothing.'

John bought some wine and poured it into each glass for them both. A couple with local looks and attire came over and sat by Michael and Gerty. John and the girl were talking then came over and sat with them. A waiter followed with more wine and nibbles.

Gerty looked at John, then Michael and then the couple.

Michael asked John, 'what is this?'

John said, 'I have asked you both here because Esther, my girlfriend (Esther nodded upon the introduction) and her family want to talk to you about us getting married.'

Gerty was astounded and said angrily, 'where's the bathroom.'

John replied inside to the right in the far corner. Gerty needed time out. She felt that she had been put on the spot. She did not even know the girl or family. In fact, she did not even know John was courting anyone.

Michael stood up and said, 'John, I had better see if your Mom's all right.'

Michael stood outside the ladies and waited for her to come out. When she did, she was a little more under control but felt so fiery.

Michael walked up to her and said even though he knew the answer, 'did you know about this?'

'I know as much as you. Zilch, nothing, knout.'

'What are we going to do?'

'Strangle the little bastard.'

Michael chuckled, 'yes, but not a good idea here.'

'I thought you had set something up through John to have a lovely romantic night out and maybe ask me something special or you had some exciting news, like a new business venture.'

'Me too but from you.'

'What are we going to do? I am so angry at the, the, the son.'

'Yes, me too but he has done it all the same. Let's go back to the table and discuss their plans calmly and then batter him when we get home?'

'I want to batter him now, please.'

Gerty was in a body of rage but knew it was not the parent of Esther's fault. She decided to play it that she knew and that the wedding plans needed to be arranged.

Gerty and Michael smiled and sat down on their allocated seats.

John leaned over and whispered to his Mom, 'are you all right?'

Gerty whispered back, 'we will talk later before I kill you, ok?'

John never answered. Esther's Mom asked in fluent English, 'are you all right?'

Gerty asked out loud to John and Esther, 'are you pregnant?'

Esther's Mom growled, 'certainly not.'

Esther's Dad asked, 'well, are you?'

John said, 'no nothing like that. We thought it a good idea for you parents to get together so we can talk about Esther and me getting hitched.'

Gerty looked at Esther's parents and asked, 'did you know about this?'

Esther's mother put her arms out and shrugged her shoulders.

Esther's father growled, 'no, not an inkling.'

Gerty responded and asked, 'what were you pair thinking? How the hell do we talk about the marriage of you two when neither family has met?'

John replied, 'Mom that's the whole idea. You parents being told at the same time about our intentions.'

Michael seemed in disbelief, and astounded said, 'wouldn't it have been a good idea for all of us to have got to know each other first and then this get together?'

John replied, 'you keep out of this.'

Michael got up and walked away. Gerty got up and apologised for her son's behaviour and went over to Michael. He walked over to some railings and leaned over to watch the glistening lights from where he was standing bounce around the ocean shore. It was all so quiet with the gentle trickles of the waves caressing the sand in and out. Michael had been hurt. He had only ever offered his support to John but John had never really forgiven him for walking out the first time.

Gerty softly said, 'D'you want to go home? I'm sorry for all this. I'll call a taxi?'

Michael replied, 'it's not your fault. John and I still have issues. I thought over time it had been worked out and he had moved on, but apparently not. John and I have some unfinished business I know, but this is not the place or the time. Let's just go back and find out what these youngsters are up to.'

Gerty looked at him in the face and softly said, 'I really do love you, you know. They just want to be together and they look to be in love, don't they?'

Michael replied softly, 'but not as much as you and I, my princess.'

With that, he kissed her passionately and arm in arm they walked back and sat down at the table. Esther's parents had stood up and were about to leave. Michael asked, 'we should at least give them a chance to tell us what this night is all about and the reason we know is for these lovers to get married, but have you told us all, John?' John was still sitting with a look of defeat.

John said, 'our intention was to tell you we are very much in love and want to get married. The other part of tonight was to ask your blessing. There is another problem that we wanted to discuss with all of you and that is our future.'

John turned to Esther and she carried on, 'Mom and Dad, we know you are struggling with this business and that we love working with you but if you don't find some hard cash soon you will lose our heritage and our future. We have a plan for both if you would listen.'

Esther's Mom and Dad married very young and took over running their family business as her inheritance. Her parents had long since passed away and the business had been going along quite pleasantly for decades. As time went by and Esther came along the economy changed and the business started to struggle. Esther's father became depressed and found it all too much. Esther tried with her minimal experience to try to pull the business together but with little backing. Esther's father was English and met Esther's Mom on a family holiday in Corfu.

Esther's Mom and Dad got up and left. They were so embarrassed to air their financial problems in public and to people they had never met. They also told Esther and John to never see each other again. They never even said good-bye; they just went back into the restaurant not to be seen again that night. John was also sacked from his job at the restaurant.

Gerty called a taxi and Michael with John went home. Nobody said a word. The next day John kept away. Michael avoided any confrontation with John and Gerty was just too furious to talk to anybody.

Without anybody knowing, Michael went and saw Esther's parents and persuaded them to sell him part of their business because they basically were in that much trouble financially he bailed them out. This was on the understanding that John or Esther had nothing to do with it. This was agreed. What nobody knew was that John and Esther were still seeing each other and planned to get married with or without anybodies consent.

It took a little over a month before John could discuss anything. He got another job at another restaurant and within eighteen months became assistant Manager. He was a grafter and had a flair for the restaurant trade. John decided as well, it was time for him to move out and rent his own place. Gerty by chance bumped into Esther's Mom while she was on a shopping trip in town.

Esther's Mom said, 'hello, I hear your son is moving out and into rented accommodation with my daughter?'

Gerty was flabbergasted because she knew nothing.

Gerty replied, 'I didn't even know he was moving out. Since the night we met I haven't really spoken to him.'

Esther's Mom said, 'your son is still planning to marry my daughter. They are in love.'

Gerty replied, 'I am sorry about that night. My son was out of order and he should have spoken to me first.'

Esther's Mom replied, 'yes he should have but he's young and most are stupid and don't think at that age. We were embarrassed because we tried to keep our business affairs with the family only and felt he was telling Sidari we had failed as restaurateurs.'

Gerty sadly said, 'yes I know, but that was not his intention.'

Esther's Mother smiled and said, 'yes, I know that now.'

Gerty replied, 'I think they will get married with or without us. Isn't it better with our blessing than without?'

Esther's Mom said, 'yes, but what can we do about it?'

Gerty suddenly had a plan. Gerty said, 'can we get together and discuss this maybe at your restaurant tomorrow?'

Esther's Mom grinned and replied, 'that would be a splendid idea.'

When Gerty got home, she waited until John got in and asked him to come into the kitchen. John obliged.

Gerty asked if he wanted a coffee and he replied, 'yes.'

Gerty asked, 'how are you?'

'Ok.'

John didn't know where to start or what to say. He felt he should keep his world to himself as he messed up so much previously.

Gerty asked, 'how's Esther?'

John glared and replied, 'what do you care?'

'Contrary to your mindless thoughts I actually care about you and your future. The plan you had was good and had structure but your implementation was crap.'

'Can I go now?'

'No, drink your coffee.'

You could have cut the atmosphere with a knife.

Gerty carried on, 'I know you are still seeing Esther and I know you still intend marrying her.'

'Yes, well, why ask?'

Gerty said sadly, 'John, I don't want to fight. I am on your side. I want to help but not in a hurtful, thoughtless way. How can I help you?'

'We have it all in hand.'

'What in hand?'

'We are going to do it our way with no help from anybody. It's just gonna take longer.'

Gerty was appalled at his attitude and asked, 'do you think we don't care? Are we horrible people that you can't talk to? Have you no trust in us?'

John replied, 'yes and no. Look, I ballsed up and am paying the price. I was hoping that our plans would be straight forward but you meddlers complicate everything.'

Gerty retorted, 'you upset Esther's parents and embarrassed not only them but us too. If you had had the courage to talk it over with Michael and me, then none of this would have happened.'

John replied, 'yes, alright, I know. No worries. We're doing it without your help.'

He then stormed out of the room and up to his bedroom. Gerty felt she had stepped on a land mine of emotion and let it go.

The next day John came into the kitchen and asked if Esther could come round for dinner at about seven. Gerty and Michael were happily gob smacked.

John left the building and Gerty looked at Michael and said, 'he might just be starting to grow up. Michael pulled Gerty to his chest and said thank god for that.'

BETRAYED

Gerty met with Esther's Mom and they discussed their children's wedding plans. Even though the couple wanted to get married in secret as defiance, the Mom's were not going to let that happen. They decided to turn detective and found out what church, what day and time the wedding was booked for. That's all they needed. Even Joe was in on the secret adventure and found out who was going to be the ushers and who was going to be there. Gerty had made friends with Esther over the times she came round for dinners plus to stay with John. They eventually moved into their two bed roomed apartment with a gorgeous sea view and made it a very cosy love nest with the help of Gerty's flair and imagination. Esther wanted a family wedding and in her own way persuaded John to succumb to a family wedding after all. Everything was already set up. Esther's

Mom had booked the restaurant for their daughter's big day and bought all the food to celebrate. Gerty had bought beautiful arrays of spectacular arrangements of flowers for the church and restaurant. Gerty had also paid the vicar of the church to ring the bells for their special day. A vintage car was embellished with ribbons to match the ivory of Esther's dress and the orange of her bouquet. All that was left to do was to buy the bride and groom their wedding present.

The next day Gerty went shopping for her son's wedding present. She thought, as she dreamed along the high street, maybe they could do with a special oil painting to match in with their flat decor, uuummmmmmmm. Then she thought perhaps a bread maker. Esther loved cooking all sorts of things. Maybe they would need a boxed cutlery set and thought that very British. Do they need a dryer and then thought not really needed in this climate? That made her chuckle to think of such a stupid thing. She gazed into a few shop windows and pondered on the idea that it would suddenly come to her as she browsed.

She heard a whisper of her name and thought perhaps it was the wind. She carried on in her own little world. She heard a pssssssssssssst and then again her name. She looked all around and saw nothing. She heard it again only louder this time. There was a small narrow alley way and she saw a shadow asking her quietly to go to it. She was intrigued and slowly walked the way of the hand waving. As she got closer, she decided it could be danger time but it was too late. Her ex-husband grabbed her arm and then pressed against her waist until she could not escape. With a firm, solid grasp, he whispered in her face. 'Hi, pretty slut. Long time no see.'

Naturally, she tried to scream, 'let me go.'

But she knew his strength was no match for her tiny frame. The nightmare had come back with a vengeance and he was in no mood to let go. He needed to play his control game first.

Gerty started to hit out at him but he only laughed and held both hands together behind her. He was a big muscly thug with shovels for hands and a build to be scared, very scared of.

'When I heard of the wedding, I knew I would see my little slut bitch again.'

Holding onto both her hands with his one hand, he slid his other hand in-between her legs and felt for her knickers. In-between the crotch he dabbled in finding her warm virginal cavity, and slid a couple of fingers inside. With his continual smile showing his huge yellow teeth, that followed with bad breath to boot. He whispered, 'I want you wet, for old time's sake. Do you remember my stonking mass of man pleasure that you used to love and lick?'

Gerty did not answer. Her head was saying hurry up and get it over with. She knew from old that it was no use fighting. She tried to look away and just wait for time to pass.

After a wriggle or two she orgasmed. He ripped her gusset and felt the entrance, with a push he was in.

'Umm, nice and warm slut. No, no playing up now. I will let go of your hands but if you move I will have to pull all your hair out now.'

Gerty stayed terrified and froze for his convenience. He played her like a doll. The motion was sickening and the orgasm a relief. Her nipples were hurting. He had bitten them while raping her and left sucker marks all around the tender flesh. He went limp almost immediately and pulled out.

'That was nice, just like old times. Must do it again soon, Gerty. You owe me big time bitch. I got you the punters and you gave me nothing.'

He grabbed her throat and lifted her to the wall. Its payback dirty Gerty and I will be collecting soon.'

With that threat, He zipped himself up, dusted himself down and left Gerty lent against the wall, motionless. She felt so helpless. She could not go to the police, she could not tell anybody because there would be more trouble. It had to be her secret. Just another to her list of hush, hushes.

Gerty sat on the floor in the alleyway for about an hour. She knew nobody would miss her because she was out shopping and shopping time could be any duration.

The day was trying to turn into night and some of the shops were closing. The evening shops were getting ready for tourists to come out and play. Gerty found a coffee shop that she did not go in usually and went straight to the toilet. As she went through, she asked for a coffee and pointed to where she was going. They acknowledged and waited to serve her when she came out again. She sat in a secluded corner away from anybody. She was lucky enough not to have any marks on her face or anywhere anybody could see them at a glance. It was very difficult to try to act normal because trauma makes you feel destroyed inside. She became a shell of nothingness. After coming back into thinking about why she was out in the first place, she realised she needed to go home with some kind of shopping, but what? The one thing they would need was money, so she decided when she got home to write them both out a nice fat cheque for their future together. That was also a relief because she did not have to force herself trying to look for something pleasant when she felt so shitty.

Gerty's ex-husband turned up out of the blue with no warning. He stood at the front door wanting to talk to Gerty. Gerty refused to see him and he was told to go away. This man was vicious. He went around the back of the property and climbed the wall. Gerty was gardening and her ex grabbed her from behind and dragged her into the garden shed. Nobody saw him there and nobody else was in the garden. This was the man that battered her black and blue, then fed her for prostitution to his mates. His mates took it in turns to humiliate her. At first his mates thought it was a joke and a bit of tantalizing fun but as time went by the violence got worse and the injuries got more intense, so much so that he broke one of her legs and ribs. When they were in the shed where he again, raped her. He then asked where his boys were. Gerty didn't say a word she just glared at him with no emotion. She was scared to death of him and knew the only way to survive his abuse was silence. His name was Marlon and he was built like a brick shit house, with the temperament to go with it. Joe came into the garden called for his Mom to come and have lunch.

Marlon put his hands to her face and one finger to his lip and whispered, 'shhh.'

When Joe went back inside to look elsewhere's for his Mom, Marlon said quietly, 'I will be back. I want to see my son's and you owe me money, bitch.'

With that in mind, he fled the same way he came over the wall. Gerty fell to the floor of the shed and could not control her emotions. The present, past and future terrified her. The rape of now, yester year and what was he going to do next. He put her in a chicken chasing mood. Michael was in the house and came into the garden. By this time everyone in the house was looking for her. Michael opened the shed and saw his precious soul mate on the floor in a heap of sorrow and despair.

Michael bent down to pick her up and asked quietly but with a disturbed voice, 'what happened to you? Has Marlon been here? What has he done to you? How did he get in? I'm gonna kill him.'

Gerty replied, 'I need to get out of here. Phone me a taxi; I need to get to the airport. Find my boys. We need to leave. Pack me a suitcase. Where can we go? I know we will go to the Canary Islands, nobody knows us there.'

Michael carefully got her up from the floor and into their bedroom. All the time she was rambling about getting out of the country and getting everyone out of danger. Michael knew she was in shock and needed a doctor to calm her down with some strong calming drugs. Beth called the doctor and he came within ten minutes. Gerty was in the shower when he came and was wrapped by her Mom in a bathrobe.

As soon as the doctor walked in she ripped off her bath robe lay on the bed with her legs wide open for all to see her naked body and said with a glassy smile, 'come on take me. Who's next to fuck me dry and make me high.'

Michael quickly covered her modesty and Beth sat by her side. The doctor talked to her but she was none coherent. Gerty kept going on about getting to another country and running away still. The doctor injected her with a strong sedative and told the rest of the family to keep a close eye on her. Next morning Beth asked Michael to come into the kitchen. In the kitchen Beth said, 'I remember the days when she would come home with bruises as big as your fist from that animal. I remember too the boys had the same. Michael they were all frightened of him. I can't understand how he found out about us living here. Somebody must have told him. One thing I don't want is you getting hurt. Marlon is a psychopath and ruthless. He would kill you just because you have his girl, even now, Michael. He has always said he owns Gerty.'

Michael said, 'he raped her in our back garden. How am I supposed to feel? I can't just let it happen. I have mates that will punish him for what he's done and I intend to call in lots of favours for my girl.'

Beth said, 'Michael just be careful you are on his victims list as well as us.'

Joe over heard some of the conversation and said, 'I bet John has got something to do with this.'

With that in mind, Michael sped out the front door. He raced to where John was working and called him outside.

John said, 'I'm working, what D'you want?'

'Have you got in contact with your Dad?'

'Yes, you told me to.'

'No I didn't. I asked if he was going.'

'You ordered me to get him here.'

'You little shit. I didn't.'

'You fucking well did.'

'Don't you dare tell anybody, or I'll make sure your family never live to talk to anybody ever again. GOT IT!'

'Yes, ok, ok. I am hearing you. Calm down. He's offered to be my best man at my wedding. I asked him over here. He is my Dad after all.'

Michael screamed, 'you want to see what he's done to your mother.'

Michael then walked away. John stood still and asked, 'what, my Dad, what D'you mean?'

The wedding was a week away. John let his father share the flat with them. Esther was a little wary but accepted that it was John's father after all. John went to work and Esther cooked breakfast for herself and John's father. Half way through cooking John's father walked up close to the cooker and looked Esther in the eye and asked if he could lend a hand. Esther backed off and told him to sit down all was in hand. He looked at her hair and told her what beautiful eyes she had. She told him to go and sit down.

He pinned her up against the kitchen units, lifted her skirt, and said, 'I want to know, are you going to be a good fuck for my son.'

By this time, he had put both her hands behind her back and pushed his penis into her soft skin. She yelped with pain and told him to take it out of her but he kept on pumping until he exploded inside her. He still held her hands and with the other played around with her nipples. She was in shock, horror and traumatised. He stepped back and put his limp tool back in his pants. Esther was a statue and couldn't believe what had just happened. She couldn't believe she had let herself be raped by this sadistic piece of shit. She was scared witless to move just in case he did something else to her.

He stuck his fingers in her vagina and said raunchily, 'you tell my son and I'll kill you. You tell anybody else and I'll tell them we've done this many times before. Oh and by the way you're a good fuck for my son.'

With that, he walked away and sat down. He growled, 'where's my breakfast, bitch.'

Esther made him breakfast but couldn't stop shaking. Marlon told her to lighten up or he would have to do it again. After eating his breakfast he walked out without a word and left Esther to it. The first thing Esther did was go to her parent's house and showered. She scrubbed like she had insects all over her body. When she had finished she had scrubbing sores all over her body. She tried to act normal and went to the restaurant as usual. She was very quiet. She was terrified just in case John's father told John and she would lose the love of her life. She also knew she did not want to go back to the apartment knowing Marlon would be there but she had no choice. Marlon had put her in an impossible situation. She went to John's restaurant and thought she would walk home with him. That meant that she would not walk into the apartment on her own. Unfortunately for her John had already left. The apartment was not far away and she walked home on her own.

John was so pleased to see her and told her he had missed her and wanted to spend the rest of the evening together but his father had arranged for just him and his Dad to go out.

Esther said, 'all right, just go.'

Esther cried the rest of the night away and wondered whether she could call off the wedding until Marlon went home. Then she thought Marlon would only make things worse. The best thing she could do was just keep everybody happy and play along. That thought made her cry even more.

A few days into the week Esther had her Hen night and all her friends met up at the local taverna. John went out with the boys for his stag night in the other direction. Marlon went with them to start but decided he wanted to be part of the pussy brigade and followed the hen party. Half way through the night, one of the girls came out of the back door drunk as a skunk.

Marlon was waiting and grabbed her by the breasts and said, 'oh yes, pussy.'

The girl just laughed and said, 'you want pussy, you show me the wild cock.'

Marlon ripped off her knickers, bent her over a bin, and put his wild cock inside her. She was laughing away and moaning at the same time.

When they had finished he said, 'what about the hen, is she ready for some virginal experimenting.

The girl replied, 'she's no virgin and it's her last night of freedom. I'll get her out so you can give her a last singles night present.'

Marlon replied, 'yee ha, bring it on.'

With that, he hid. He knew it was going to be Esther and he didn't want her to notice him or fathom out his intentions.

Esther came out alone because she thought it might be John.

She called quietly, 'John where are you?'

Esther was dressed in a flowery, long multi-coloured dress down to her knees and covered with a short red cardigan. She was suddenly swung round and horrifically confronted by Marlon. She tried to pull back and he kept grabbing her closer until he pinned her up against the wall. Esther kept on saying no, please no, but he moved her g string to one side and slid his thick stiff cock up into her cavity. Esther screamed with pain but nobody heard her. She tried to pull him off but to no avail. He rode her like a smooth horse filly and all she could do was cry.

He clenched her buttocks and pulled himself out when he had finished and said poetically,

'Soon to be wedded,

You've already been bedded,

Now all the pleasure is mine.

You fuck well girl,

Till the next time.'

He ran, leaving Esther on the floor in a pool of sperm. Her dress was covered in the stuff. She cried as she ran to the toilet, desperately wiping at herself, trying to rid herself of the mess and emotional trauma. She sat on the toilet sobbing, not knowing what to do. The other girl that set her up came into find her.

She said, 'I told you there was a surprise waiting for you. Did you get it?'

Esther screamed and rushed out of the toilet. She grabbed the girl by the neck and squeezed her so tight she could hardly breathe. Another girl friend came in and pulled Esther off of her. Esther could hardly see anybody with all her crying. All her friends ended up in the toilet asking what had happened.

Esther said, 'I have been raped and this dick set me up.'

The girl said, 'it was only a joke. I never meant any harm.'

One of the girlfriends said, 'let's go to the police?'

Esther replied, 'no.'

Another asked, 'why don't you want to go to the police, you've been raped?'

Esther replied, 'no, it's complicated.'

Another girl said, 'complicated, what's complicated about rape?'

Esther replied, 'come on let's get out of here.'

Esther got so drunk that her friends had to carry her back to her apartment. John had been sick and was able to stay in the restaurant he was last in. Marlon managed to get back to the apartment and saw Esther sprawled out on the bed. Before Esther noticed, he had her pinned down and ripped her clothes off. She laid naked with her legs apart and Marlon in his shagging position. This time his shear weight kept her from moving. He also played, massaging her breasts, while working over the soil, inside her yet again.

Esther was getting sick of this and said, 'why don't you fuck off and leave us alone, you bastard.'

As he pushed and pulled his dick inside her he replied, 'now don't talk to your father in law like that.'

Esther said, 'just fuck off.'

Marlon replied, 'I'm doing my best. Hang on.'

He got off and turned her over onto her knees then rammed her with his cock into her vagina and held her breasts in both hands. He kept on going. Esther had no choice but to do as she was told. He was in full control. His sheer size inside and out dictated how she would kneel and move in with the rhythm or she would get hurt.

John walked into the bedroom and saw the picture. He was too pissed to do anything.

He just grunted, 'the weddings off.'

He then collapsed into a sick pile and fell asleep. When he woke up he found himself on his own. He thought he had just had a night mare and what he saw was not real. It was just his imagination playing tricks with his drunken state. He also did not know what time it was and panic set in. He realised that for his wedding day he needed to be at home with his Mom as they were to help him get ready. He raced to his Mom's and found everyone was walking around as if nothing was happening today.

John said, 'it's my wedding day, is anyone going to help me get ready?'

Michael walked passed and said, 'like fuck.'

Joe walked passed and asked, 'have you seen Mom yet John?'

Beth and Trevor stood by the doorway and said, 'how's your father. Is he dead yet?'

John replied, 'that's a terrible thing to say.'

John thought for a minute, 'where is my father?'

John went to his Mom's room only to find her still in bed and fast asleep.

Michael came up behind him and said, 'leave her alone. She's not well.'

John asked, 'what's wrong with her?'

Michael said, 'she has been raped by your father, yet again and she has been traumatised by that bastard.'

John backed off and went down stairs. John asked, 'Grandma, what's going on?'

Beth retorted quite calmly, 'your father is what's happened. You invited him here and now he has destroyed people's lives. It's all on your head, John. I hope you're proud of yourself.'

With that, she walked away. Trevor came out and asked John, 'what were you thinking bringing that shyster back into our lives? You know what he did to you, your Mom, and your little brother.'

John replied, 'but he told me he's changed, he's not the man he was, and he is now a religious man that follows Christ.'

Trevor retorted, 'the devil more like. He brings with him nothing but destruction. John, tell him to go home.'

Esther burst into the house. John in his wisdom had left the front door open. She was in a state and asked Beth where Gerty was?

Beth said, 'asleep upstairs and was in no mood to be disturbed.'

Esther ran quickly up the stairs to her room. She opened the door and tried to wake Gerty up but she was too heavily sedated to get any acknowledgement. Esther burst into tears and sat on the end of the bed.

Michael came in and spoke quietly, 'Esther, what's wrong. Has John's Dad got to you as well?'

She glared a victim's glare and the tears just gushed with no sound. She got up and suddenly thought of her friend, Rosa. Her body used it's might for the next point of action and sped down the stairs, knocking Michael in the process as she flew past. Michael looked at Gerty pitifully as she slept thinking he could have saved her. He should have done something. He let her down. He quietly closed the door and went down stairs. John was sitting in the kitchen on his own. Nobody wanted any contact with him and his thoughtlessness. Michael made a cup of coffee and walked out into the lounge without saying a word. The atmosphere could have been cut with a knife.

The wedding was to take place at midday in the church at the top of the hill. Esther had endured enough of his abuse and wanted her sweet revenge. When she got to Rosa she had a plan and felt a little more positive. Rosa was in one of the letting apartments tidying up.

Esther swung round the door and asked, 'Rosa, can I talk to you?'

Rosa could see that something had happened and replied, 'yes, my apartment is open. Go make us both a coffee. I will be with you in a minute.'

Esther did just that. Rosa finished what she was doing and met Esther in her apartment. Rosa sat down and Esther passed the coffee over.

Rosa looked at Esther and said, 'what the hell has happened to you. You're supposed to be getting married today. Why aren't you getting ready? Esther started crying again. When Rosa looked at Esther a little closer she noticed bits of her clothes were torn. Esther blurted everything out that had happened to her in such a short space of time. She also told her about Gerty and how it affected her. By the time Esther had finished telling her all, Rosa was furious. Rosa asked, 'have you got a plan for this heathen?'

'Yes, but it has it's risks.'

'I like the unknown, tell me your plan.'

After an hour of planning, discussing, re-planning, discussing and finally coming to an agreement of what they were going to do, Esther went to prepare herself for her wedding day.

THE WEDDING PLANS

———◆———

Esther knew if this was going to work, she needed to be looking good and feeling as great as she possibly could under the circumstances. When she got to her Mom's house, she rushed upstairs into her old bedroom where all was laid out for her convenience. Her Mom came into the bedroom while Esther was in the shower and asked if all was all right.

Esther replied, 'no problem. Is everything ready?'

Esther's Mom said, 'as ready as it's ever gonna be. I am just going to get ready myself. I will be back in about ten minutes, Ok?'

Esther shouted over the shower noise, 'ok.'

A knock came at the door and it was Rosa. She looked gorgeous in her new chiffon cream with dainty flowers floaty dress. She also had a wrap in baby pink. Her hat was a lacy affair with a baby pink ribbon wrapped around to match her wrap. Her two inch high heels in a court shoe fashion were cream to match her dress. She looked very sexy with her luscious long legs and a face like an angel. She was dressed for action and knew it. Rosa asked if she could go up stairs and help Esther get ready.

Her father said, 'yes, of course. Second bedroom on the left.'

Esther was sitting on the bed trying to dry her hair.

Rosa noticed a big bruise appearing on Esther's left shoulder and said, 'we need to disguise that somehow.'

Esther glared at Rosa and said, 'this has got to work. We only have one chance at this, you do realise?'

Esther's Mom walked into the room and said, 'you can always change your mind. You don't have to do this.'

Her Mom was obviously thinking about the wedding and not the revenge.

The car turned up outside waiting for Esther's departure. Esther's Mom was faffing about with flowers for button holes. Esther's Dad was talking to the chauffeur. The rest of Esther's brothers and sisters were waiting at the church.

Esther had a sudden, very worrying thought, 'where was Marlon?'

She phoned Michael and he told her that John was with them and John said his father was supposed to be at their apartment getting ready. Either way they would meet him at the church. Esther started to tremble. Just thinking about that cretin made her blood crawl. When she got off the phone, she said to Rosa, 'all is in order and we will meet every body at the church.'

Rosa looked questioningly at Esther and re iterated, 'as planned, right?'

Esther nodded her acknowledgement.

Esther was ready; she walked down the stairs and dripped gorgeousness. Her ivory wedding dress revelled in innocence and portrayed a woman going on a new journey into a married life. Her Father saw an angel of purity standing before him and tears rolled down his cheeks. He remembered his little girl of yester year and how he shared precious moments with her and the family. Moments in time to capture and treasure. He saw the funny innocents of a child needing guidance, love and understanding. He did not want to let go but knew she had to move forward to blossom and grow. Her Mom felt the same and held back the tears for the church. Her father held her arm and guided her to the car. Her Mother and Rosa went in the car behind.

Esther gave Rosa a small bag and told her to take it with her to the church. Rosa knew what was inside but her puzzled mother did not.

The chauffeur took them the long way round. The summer had arrived with a rushed cold wind and rain. At the church front door on the wedding day, a beautiful array of warmth and sunshine erupted just in time. Outside the church when they arrived were the ushers, brothers, and sisters of Esther and the massive Marlon. He was done up like a dogs dinner. Proud of what he looked like and giving the big I am stance of look at me, I am a wild stallion to be admired by all who purveyed.

One of Esther's sisters came over to her as Esther was getting out of the car and said, 'John isn't here yet. Go around again.'

Esther kept getting out of the car.

She replied, 'I am getting out and we will wait for him to arrive.'

Esther's father said, 'but he's not here? We can go around again and wait for him to come?'

Esther carried on with, 'no that's all right, we'll wait inside.'

Esther's Father was flabbergasted and did as he was told.

Rosa and Esther's Mother came rushing round to Esther's aid and her Mother tried to persuade her to get back into the car but to no avail. Rosa suddenly became the bridesmaid on Esther's request. Esther with bouquet in hand glided slowly with Rosa behind up to the church front steps. Just inside the church doors was standing Marlon. He looked a little hesitant, as his Groom was nowhere to be seen.

Marlon looked at Esther and proudly expressed, 'you look gorgeous. My son is a lucky fella.'

Esther with a controlled smile looked Marlon in the eye and whispered, 'can I have a word with you before the wedding ceremony?'

Marlon bowed his head at Esther's Parents and replied, 'certainly.'

Esther whispered again to Marlon, 'then follow me.'

Esther walked slowly down the aisle and met the Vicar standing at the altar. The Vicar who was going to perform the ceremony asked where the groom was.

Esther bent forward and said to the Vicar, 'is there a very private room where I might wait until he does arrive?'

The Vicar thought this quite unusual but replied quietly, almost a whisper, 'follow me.'

Marlon went first, then Esther and then Rosa. Esther asked the Vicar if they could be alone and he obliged.

The Vicar left them to it. Marlon said, 'my, this is cosy two young ladies at my disposal.'

He walked up to Rosa and said, 'I haven't had the pleasure. You are?'

Rosa replied, 'you might if you play your cards right.'

Marlon's eyes nearly popped out of his head. Marlon put his hands on the cheeks of Rosa's bum and said, 'would you like a quickie now?'

Esther stood one side of him while Rosa played him on the other side. Esther put her hand on Marlon's shoulder and Rosa did the same on his other.

Rosa smiled seductively and said, 'ready?'

Esther smiled seductively as she glanced at Rosa and replied, 'ready.'

They both pushed the injections into the shoulders of Marlon. He felt the sharp pains and turned away from them rapidly.

He growled, 'what have you given me, you bitches.'

Esther smiled seductively again and said, 'Marlon, this won't take long.'

Rosa said with her seductive smile of elation, 'this is the quickie you were on about.'

Esther said, 'but this time it's on our terms. Enjoy.'

Rosa said to Marlon, 'enjoy.'

Marlon hit the deck. His muscles went limp. He could do nothing. His whole being was paralysed. He was in submission. The only way they knew he was scared was because of his eyes. They moved vigorously around the room and he blinked in terror. Esther took off her wedding dress and stripped to nakedness. In her bag of tricks that Rosa carried down the aisle were some clothes and a knife, plus a large pair of scissors. Esther got dressed into her jeans and a cotton top. She also changed her shoes to pumps. Rosa stayed the same.

The girls took all his clothes off, rolled Marlon onto his back and put him on a sheet of bed linen. When face down they bound him so that they could also hang him from something. They proceeded to tie his ankles together with a bit of vestry rope found disguarded in a corner. Rosa then took out the large scissors and with one hand holding his limp penis, pushed the pointed end down the shaft of his bell end. While this was going on Marlon's eyes began to cry tears and his eye lashes were blinking profusely. His eyes expressed pain, and lots of it. The scissors were long and sharp and blood oozed out of the top of his bell end. Rosa squeezed the scissor ends together until one reached the other. She could see the muscle of the penis split with the secretion of blood.

Now the other side but before she did this she saw Esther rubbing his brow saying, 'there, there. It will all be over soon my father in law to be.'

Rosa carried on doing the other side until Marlon's penis looked like it was a banana that had just been peeled. He bled quite a lot and Rosa found she had blood on parts of her dress.

Esther said, 'now we need to get him down these stairs.'

Rosa replied, 'I got it.'

With the sheet, they both heaved him close to the step then with a huge kick, he rolled down the steps to the bottom. The steps lead down to the river cavern from the ocean that ran under the church.

Esther said, 'we had better hurry up. They will be wondering where we are.'

Rosa replied, 'all right, all right, nearly there.'

Marlon was bashed and bruised but it was only superficial. They rolled him to the river's edge, tied the rope from his hands to a metal pole sticking out of the water on their side and pushed him into the water. He sunk straight away and because the tide was in, covered him. They would have to come back later though to make sure he was dead.

Both girls dashed up stairs. The Vicar was calling for some kind of sign that all was well.

Esther shouted, 'we're coming.'

Rosa quickly washed the blood off the stone floor with Esther's jeans and the top was used to mop up other bits around the vestry. Esther got dressed into her wedding gown again and Rosa got most of the blood off her dress.

They both walked out and Esther said to her friends and neighbours, 'I've been stood up,' and ran along the aisle and into the car. She sat there crying whilst Rosa asked Esther's father to take her home.

Esther's mother was so distraught with what had happened she said to Rosa, 'where's Marlon?'

Rosa replied, 'He went to find John and give him a piece of his mind.'

She accepted that and both got in the second car. The guests were left to their own devices and left the church.

TIME TO TIDY UP

Next day after all the commotion Rosa went round to Esther's house and they both carried on their plans. They knew that not many people would be in the church and so went in the front entry, up the aisle, into the vestry and down the steps where they pushed Mister Fuck wit to his demise. Marlon was not far from being dead. His penis was no more. It had been eaten away by rats. He had almost bled to death. The rape drug had worn off and he was able to speak. He begged them to kill him properly but the girls wanted every pound of aching flesh to feel the pain they went through when he helped himself to their bodies, not once but twice.

Rosa said smiling innocently at him, 'we can't kill you because we are not murderers.'

Marlon suddenly found all his strength to get free and screeched, 'you bastard bitches, I'll get you for this.'

Esther said with a knife in her hands, 'I have a message from Gerty to you.'

As she said this, she plunged the knife into his chest, pulled it out a plunged again.

She then said, 'Gerty said, she will miss you Mr X and hope you live in hell.'

With that, he gasped his last breath.

A huge boulder was tied to his midriff and they rolled him into the river and watched his body sink about six feet down. The sun's rays did not enter that part of the river and so nobody would ever see his body again, unless he somehow got free.

After leaving Marlon dead, they went to visit Gerty. Gerty was up and Michael was trying to persuade her to have some breakfast.

Esther asked if John was around so she could talk to him.

Michael said, 'John was in the garden.'

Esther went out and smiled at him.

She said, 'Hi John. You never turned up at our wedding. Why is that?'

'I saw you have sex with my Dad. How could you?'

Esther retorted, 'your father raped me, not once but twice. No, in fact three times. How dare you say that? Your father raped a few women around here including your mother, twice. What kind of a man invites a rapist to his wedding? I never ever, ever want to see you, talk to you, or even be in the same room as you, ever again.'

With that, she walked away and joined them in the kitchen.

Esther said, 'you know that Marlon, you were married to many years ago?'

Gerty started shaking and looked at Esther while she was talking.

Esther carried on, 'he's dead. The fucker is in hell and is dead.'

Gerty's tears welled inside her and then down her cheeks. She flung her arms around Esther and hugged her for ages.

Gerty said, 'thank you god for everything.'

John came into the room to apologise and Gerty said, 'I loved you as a son. I hate you as a man. Get out and never come back into our lives. You are not my son anymore.'

John turned around and simply left.

Time settled its ugly head and months went past. Esther found she was pregnant with Marlon's baby. She got rid of it. Her life stabilised. She spent all her time helping her parents run the restaurant. Boys were definitely off the list of wants, needs and cravings. Instead she stuck to food, eating, cooking, creating and baking. Rosa became her best friend.

Time does heal but not the way you would expect sometimes. The nasty taste of hurt stays the longest. The game of will it ever come back plays its anxious cards. The deck of cards hands out all sorts of trivia, and with experience yet again, we handle the assortment of quandaries. Life can be very kind but difficult, to be handled with care, consideration and sometimes bloody mindedness. Either way no matter what you have to do, what is right for you is the ultimate challenge.

GERTY'S YEARNING

Years went by and Bella kept in touch but Gerty always felt she should have been part of her own business. She felt she had neglected Bella in many ways to gratify her own world. Bella did not know the in's and out's of what had happened to Gerty over the years but thought that Gerty had changed. She had changed in a way that she had lost her identity and well being.

One afternoon while talking business on the phone Bella asked, 'why don't ya com fer a break, spend som time wid us. Dat would be a nice treat for der girlies.'

Gerty wanted to but did not want Michael to know she was going to The Passion Flower Club. She told Bella she would think about it.

A month went past and the winter was well on its way. Frequent thunderstorms lit up the skies with many electrical arrays of thick and thin jagged lines reaching from one side of the sky to the other. They seemed far more intense, louder, and scarier. The wind howled carrying the cold with it and so too were the crashing waves of the ocean.

Gerty asked Michael, 'would you mind me going to England for about three weeks. I need to check on a few things and catch up with a few friends. I would also like to shop in London. I know how you hate shopping.'

'No. Three weeks is a long time but I am sure absence makes the heart grow fonder. Will you be alright on your own though?'

'I don't know, but I would like to go.'

'Yeah, why not. Maybe I could stay a few nights at our Hotel and check how it is getting on. Somebody told me that things are not as they should be.'

'Well, that sounds like a plan then?'

'Definitely.'

The usual flights were booked and Bella sent a taxi for Gerty to be picked up. When she arrived at the Club, Bella and the girls had splashed out on a welcoming party for Gerty, after all she was the owner. Gerty was a little taken aback but none the less saw many familiar faces and more new ones.

Gerty mingled and spoke to so many people. She soon became familiar with her business enterprise. She didn't realise that there were so many clients and business was booming. She only ever saw the profits that kept going into her bank account year after year. She got Bella to one side and kissed her on her cheek.

'Bella thank you for all you have done. Without you this place would not be here now.'

Bella replied as she kissed her back, 'ya git dat reet. I would not be ear if it weren't fer ya

Gerty and ya gev me a chance, girl, and I took it wid bote arms, girl.'

Frank, Gerty's old client came over and asked, 'have you got any knickers on?'

Gerty smiled and slapped him gently on his shoulder.

Gerty said with a wide grin, 'you always did tease me, didn't you? Anyway, it's a Secret.'

'Fancy a quick one for old times' sake?'

Gerty suddenly remembered the fun they used to have. Intimate chuckling about each other's little body parts. She then looked around the room and noticed a man that came to her for full English because his wife had problems down below that would deter her from personal, intimate play. Another whose wife had Dementia and he just could not be intimate with a woman that could not remember who he was most of the time. The wife's condition got worse.

Next, a thirty-year-old man came up to her and said, 'Gerty, I am married with two children now.'

'What happened?'

The man said,' you gave me confidence in the bedroom department and now I have a wife. She's beautiful.'

With all that she had gone through and experienced, there was none so acknowledging for what she was, pure and simply a prostitute. She did not flower it up nor did she splendour in her prowess. Sex could be many things to many people. Like animals, they are cherished, abused, tortured, loved, and admired. Life is full of all sorts of individuals that love, hurt, and abuse because they can. What kind of people as humans are we, she thought. As intelligent people we should embrace all things but instead we try to destroy all for what, money, want, greed or just because we can? It is far better to care and have compassion for all things. To healthily love somebody is a pleasure if reciprocated. To wallow in the arms of wholesomeness is a drug in itself.

Gerty smiled and carried on looking around. Some men she saw, just simply wanted extra sex and others found comfort in their prostitutes. Either way Gerty always knew she provided a service whether society liked it or not she loved what she did.

She reached for Frank's hand and whispered in his ear, 'come and see if I am wearing knickers or not, lover boy, 'as they brushed past the guests and rushed upstairs.

ACKNOWLEDGEMENTS

———◆———

My husband Bill Allen has been a treasure. He has helped, supported, and checked my grammar, as well as proof read. I thank you from the bottom of my heart.

My Mom, Irene Collings, supported me too in so many ways. Love you Mom. Xxxxx

Sarah Howard is a beautiful, caring lady and my niece. She has helped by reading the script and gave positive feedback. I love this woman to bits. Thanks Sar's.

To Nathan Pascal, thanks Nath for the good old giggles about my books. You gave me inspiration. Our BBQ evenings were sheer delight.

ILLUSTRATIONS

Primarily my husband, Bill Allen, created the Illustration of the book. I suggested a few colours and hey presto; our wonderful masterpiece was born.

OTHER PUBLICATIONS

Lilibat Belly Place   ISBN No. 978-1-4678-9618-4

Lilibat Lilly-Bell Place   ISBN NO. 978-1-4678-9659-7